Totally Bound Publishing books by JJ Black:

Great Lakes Wolves
Accepting the Alpha

Revelations
Ask the Oracle

I0570593

Revelations

ASK THE ORACLE

JJ BLACK

Ask the Oracle
ISBN # 978-1-78184-766-4
©Copyright JJ Black 2014
Cover Art by Posh Gosh ©Copyright April 2014
Interior text design by Claire Siemaszkiewicz
Totally Bound Publishing

Published in 2014 by Totally Bound Publishing, Newland House, The Point, Weaver Road, Lincoln, LN6 3QN, United Kingdom.

Totally Bound Publishing is an imprint of Total-E-Ntwined Limited.

ASK THE ORACLE

Dedication

For Joanna. Your endless enthusiasm and excitement
never fail to inspire me. Thank you.

Chapter One

Grayson Muir sat calmly at his desk, waiting for the interrogation to begin. With a police detective present, it was never long before the questions and accusations started to fly. There was always the initial disbelief. Thankfully, most got over it fairly quick, then the grilling began.

"How long are you going to waste my time?" Hands fisted and jaw clenched, the man sitting across the desk from him was definitely pissed off.

"Excuse me?"

"I don't know what bullshit story you sold to my captain but it was enough for him to order me down here. Personally, I don't have time for this shit. I've got a missing five-year-old girl to find and the clock is ticking. Every second I'm stuck here with you is another second the bastard who took her has to hurt her. I promised her parents I would get her back and I intend to keep that promise. Now," he growled, pushing back from Gray's desk, "if you don't mind, I've got real work to do."

"I know where she is."

The detective froze. "What?"

"The little girl—Maddie Thompson, right? I know where she is. I can help you."

"You've got to be kidding me," the detective scoffed. "You're trying to tell me that you know where Maddie Thompson is?"

"Yes, Detective. That is exactly what I'm telling you." When the older man continued to glare skeptically at him, Gray flashed him an understanding smile.

"What the fuck? Are you sure?" the detective barked, his round face flushed, his tone edging in on belligerent.

Gray bit back a laugh. It was often one of the first questions asked, and always the biggest waste of time. He was an Oracle, so of course he was sure. He understood why some were hesitant to believe. He was about as far from the stereotypical image of an Oracle as you could get. Public consensus still thought of Oracles as seventy-year-old, hunchbacked old ladies who spent their days darning socks and drinking tea. For most, the idea that a twenty-five-year-old, six-foot tall, one-hundred-eighty-pound man could be a powerful Oracle was laughable. Add to that his dark hair, emerald-green eyes and movie star good looks, and it was hard to get anyone to take him seriously on their first meeting. Thankfully, that opinion didn't last long once they'd had a chance to watch him work. If the detective had been one of his regulars, he would have known better, but since he was new, Gray decided it was only fair to cut him some slack.

"Yes, Detective Branson," Gray answered patiently. "I'm sure. You'll find the girl in a small white house just off Monroe Street. She's safe at the moment. The men who took her won't be back for a few hours, so I recommend retrieving her soon."

The detective continued to stare at him, brows furrowed, his lips pulled down into a frown.

Gray sighed. There were always a few hard sells. "If you'll give me a minute, I'll write down the address and a description of the kidnappers to aid your investigation."

Detective Branson still looked hesitant, but finally gave a nod of approval. His glare never wavered as Gray wrote down the information and handed it over. The detective scanned the sheet before looking back to him, his eyes wide.

"How could you possibly know this?" Branson's expression still held its hard edge, but a hint of bewilderment had begun to creep in.

"I'm an Oracle, Detective. I usually know a lot more than I would like to." Gray felt a bit of pity for the man as he watched the detective's eyes narrow in confusion. While there were many people who looked to Oracles with a near god-like idolization, for some, the idea of an *all-knowing* Oracle was too much to comprehend. Detective Branson was definitely one of the latter.

Taking pity on the man, Gray stood. "You should get going, Detective. It will be better for the girl if she is recovered while the men are gone. There is a small window of time. I recommend you take advantage of it." He came around the side of his desk and gestured to the door.

Hesitantly, the detective rose from his seat and followed Gray's lead. He was about to step through the doorway when he switched gears and came to an abrupt stop. When he turned back to face Gray, there was a question clearly written on his face.

Gray smiled reassuringly. "She'll be fine, Detective. At the moment, she's scared but undamaged. If you go to her now, you'll have her back before any serious harm befalls her."

It took a moment, but the detective's expression finally cleared with the understanding Gray's words conveyed. Determination replaced his previous confusion.

"Thank you for your help, Mr Muir. I won't pretend to understand how you know the things you do, but at this point I have to take a chance and believe you. I just hope you're right. It's time Maddie was back home with her family. I'll send word on how everything turns out."

With his shoulders back and his head held high, Detective Branson looked like a man ready to march into battle. The stern expression on the older man's face didn't fool Gray for a minute, but he'd let the man keep his illusions. Long ago, Gray had made it a point of practice to use his gift to evaluate all of the men and women he worked with. Some might call it an invasion of privacy. Gray thought of it as plain old common sense. While his gift could be a powerful tool for good, its lure for evil was just as strong. He had to be sure that he could trust those he worked with, both on the police force and in the private sector. Based on that evaluation, he knew the detective was one of the good guys. Despite his surly personality, Gray had never met a man who cared more deeply for the people of their city than Detective Dave Branson. Smiling softly, he offered the detective a hand, which the stern man readily accepted.

"I'd appreciate that, Detective. If there's anything else I can do to help with the investigation, don't hesitate to call. My assistant has already been informed that until this case is officially closed, it is my top priority and that you are to be immediately connected to my direct line."

Gray was a firm believer in seeing things through till the end. With his police consulting jobs, that philosophy was even more important. Cases involving children always touched close to his heart. There was no way he could walk away until he was sure he had done everything in his power to ensure the best possible ending.

Shock flashed across the detective's face, but was gone just as fast. He responded with a brisk nod and a grunt before he was out the door. Gray smiled. Making his way to out to the lobby, Gray found his assistant, Sarah, organizing paperwork for what he assumed was his next meeting. As an Oracle, his services were in constant demand. He had a waiting list six months long just to get a consultation, not to mention the freelance work he did for the police.

Oracles were very rare. There were only six known in the entire United States, each with a varying level of talent. Gray was right at the top of their ranks. He was able to see the past, present and all possible futures. It had been speculated that he was one of the most powerful Oracles in the world, but he couldn't care less. His only concern was helping as many people as he could with his 'gift'.

It had taken him a long time to see his abilities as a blessing, and not the curse that had tortured him for more than half of his life. Abandoned as an infant, he'd spent his childhood in orphanages and group homes where his visions had tormented him to the point where he'd almost taken his own life. He'd been an open channel, allowing everything to come through but without the benefit of a shutoff switch. It had been a chance meeting with Stephen Jurgens, a well-known psychic, when he was eighteen that helped him understand that he was an Oracle and not mentally deranged, as he had previously believed. The older man had become both a friend and mentor, saving his life in more ways than one. Stephen had taught him how to both strengthen and control his power. The lessons he'd learned from his friend had been invaluable. With his newly gained control, he was finally able to choose what visions and information to see, and ignore the rest. The ability to know everything truly made Gray appreciate the novelty of a real surprise, good or bad.

Now, almost eight years later, Gray had truly come to grips with what he was. He had his own consulting firm, Revelations, and business was booming. The company was small by design, made up of himself, Sarah, his accountant, Drew, and his security team. They were like a family, which was something he didn't have much experience with, but found he loved.

Sensing his approach, Sarah looked up, flashing him her usual megawatt smile. "How's it goin', handsome? Any news on the little girl?"

"Yes, ma'am. She's going to be fine. Detective Branson just left and should be on his way to get her now. With any luck, she'll be back home with her family tonight."

"Oh, thank God!" Sarah breathed. "Will they catch the guys that took her?"

"Yes," Gray growled, dangerously. "Even if I have to *See* them for the next month straight. They won't walk away from this, I promise you." Gray didn't tell Sarah that he had *Seen* what they would have done to the little girl, even after they had gotten the ransom they were demanding from her family. Sarah didn't need that kind of knowledge. It was never a good idea to let her get too curious about some of the things he had *Seen*. The what-ifs would drive a person mad. Better he be the only one to suffer the burden of knowing what could have happened.

When Sarah gave him a knowing look, he did his best not to appear guilty. Gray hated that she could see through him so well. At times, it was like she had a VIP access to his soul. She always knew when he was keeping things from her. "So, what do you have lined up for me for the rest of the afternoon?"

Sarah threw him one last suspicious glare, making it clear that he wasn't pulling anything over on her, before turning her attention back to the paperwork on her desk.

"Luckily, we've got a pretty light afternoon. Just case review and billing verification. You know...all that boring stuff that helps keep us in business." Gray's immediate scowl had Sarah laughing. Gray hated both activities and she knew it. He usually put them off as long as possible...or found a way to con Sarah into doing it for him.

He was about to try to beg off, when Sarah's phone rang. Giving her a pout, he batted his eyelashes playfully at her.

"Don't even think about it," she scowled at him sternly. "You're not getting out of it this time, *Mr Muir*. I'm not buying the cute face. Go clear off some space on your desk so we have room, while I get this call. I'll be there in five minutes and you better be ready to work, mister." Pointing her finger toward the hallway for emphasis, she answered the call with her free hand, still giving him a piercing look.

Reluctantly admitting defeat, Gray made his way back to his office. He had just started to sort through the mess that covered his desk, when his door burst open. Expecting to see Sarah, he looked up, ready to tease her about her over-the-top entry. When his eyes lifted, the sight before him left him speechless.

Instead of finding his five-foot-nothing, blonde-haired, blue-eyed assistant, he was treated to the sight of an olive-skinned, raven-haired god. The man in his doorway had to be close to seven feet of dark, dangerous and delicious. His broad, powerful body was covered in layers of thick, corded muscle that Gray had a strong desire to explore with his tongue. Long, onyx hair fell well past the middle of his back and his almond-shaped, mocha eyes were mesmerizing in their intensity. The color was amazing, like melted chocolate, but it was the hint of hellfire flickering in their depths that truly caught Gray's attention.

Demon. *Fuck! Of all the luck.*

Chapter Two

"In civilized society, it's considered polite to knock," Gray stated sardonically. He chastised himself for his initial attraction toward his Demonic intruder. It was a well-known fact that Demons were not to be trusted. He should know better. "Can I help you?"

"You are Grayson Muir." It wasn't a question. The Demon's voice was a deep, rich baritone. It brought with it thoughts of silk sheets and sweat-slick skin. Gray's breath caught and his pants became uncomfortably tight. Lust Demon. *Damn it!*

"I'm not in the mood for this shit today, Demon. If you just came here to screw with me, then you can show yourself out. I've got stuff to do." Dismissing the Demon, Gray turned his attention back to the mess that was his desk.

"My name is not Demon," the man growled, obviously insulted. "My name is Andreo Demos, but you may call me Dreo."

When Gray failed to respond, he felt the Demon's gaze on him, his appraising look so intense it was almost like a physical touch.

"You're not afraid of me?"

The disbelief in the Demon's voice was amusing, so Gray didn't bother to hide his laugh. Andreo Demos was not the first 'monster' he had met and far from the scariest. Probably the sexiest, but Gray wasn't going to tell him that. Lust Demons already thought enough of themselves — no need to throw fuel on that fire.

"No, I'm not afraid of you," Gray responded, not bothering to stop his cleaning efforts. "Now, is there something I can help you with or were you just passing through?"

The Demon frowned, confusion clouding his expression. "There is some trouble in the Underworld. Due to recent events, we have found ourselves in need of an Oracle. On behalf of the Demon Council, I would like to retain your services."

Gray stopped shuffling papers, shock rendering him frozen. He couldn't imagine what type of situation would cause a Demon to need help from an Oracle. Demons were known for being the snobs of the paranormal community. They liked to claim that they were all-powerful and therefore superior to all other paras. Gray would have assumed there was some type of Demon out there capable of *Seeing*. Well, that was just too bad for Andreo Demos. Grayson Muir didn't take on jobs for Demons.

"Thanks for the offer, but I think I'll pass."

"Excuse me?" Dreo's brow rose in disbelief.

"I said, thanks but no thanks."

"But I haven't even told you what the job is —"

"Oh, it doesn't matter," Gray said, waving a dismissive hand. "I don't take on Demon cases."

"Are you joking? Why the hell not?"

"It's a personal choice and none of your concern," Gray snapped, his voice surprisingly rough. "Just like any business, I have the right to refuse service to anyone. Therefore, I won't be working for any Demons. Now, if that's all, I have work to get back to." Gray turned away from the gorgeous Demon, hoping he would take the hint and leave before Gray's raging hormones made him do something he knew he'd hate himself for later—like beg the man to ride him into the floor.

The room went quiet. The silence was so complete, Gray was sure Dreo had left. Letting out a breath of relief, he turned—and practically jumped out of his skin at the sight of the dark-haired Demon, sitting casually on the corner of his desk. How the man had gotten so close without Gray hearing him was both baffling and terrifying.

"What are you still doing here?" he stammered, trying to calm his racing heart.

Dreo tilted his head to the side but said nothing. He stared at Gray curiously. His smoldering gaze was unsettling and filled Gray with nervous energy. He felt naked under that scrutiny, stripped bare, all his secrets on display. He didn't like the feeling—some things were private for a reason. Lips pursed, he scowled darkly at Dreo before storming over to his door. He glared pointedly at the infuriating man.

"I think it's time for you to leave."

"Why do you distrust Demons so strongly?" Dreo asked, his dark brow arched. "Make me understand so I can attempt to repair this rift between us."

Gray's body went rigid as his muscles tensed. "As I said before, it's a personal matter and nothing for you to worry yourself over. If you're in the market for an Oracle, Opal Vasquez has an office off of Pearl Street. I know for a fact that she takes on Demon clients. I can write you a referral, if you'd like." Gray made a move toward his desk but was stopped by a hand on his shoulder.

"Do you think I didn't fully research Oracles before coming to you? I didn't randomly pull your name from the phone book. I chose you because you are the best. The situation is delicate, and discretion is a must. By all accounts, your skill is rivaled only by your professionalism. I am in dire need of both."

Gray knew he should refuse outright. No good ever came from working with Demons. Unfortunately, his inherent sense of curiosity grabbed a hold of him, driving him to delve deeper into the mystery that surrounded the man before him.

"What's the job?" Even as the words crossed his lips, he knew he was going to regret asking. Sadly, he knew better than anyone that a bell can never be un-rung.

The smirk that tugged at the corner of Dreo's sensuous lips immediately made Gray nervous. When a Demon looked at you with victory in his eyes, it was a good time to be concerned.

"The Lord of the Underworld has been murdered," Dreo stated, his expression becoming serious in the blink of an eye. "Whoever is responsible was able to mask their presence. We have no idea who the guilty party is or even where to start looking. This is why we are in need of your particular skill set. The first part of the job is to identify the murderer, so they can be apprehended and—"

"Executed?" Gray asked, his tone sharp.

"Brought to justice," Dreo continued, brow arched.

"Yeah, right," Gray scoffed. "I have a pretty good understanding of how Demons administer *justice*." Grabbing a stack of papers, he began to shuffle through them angrily.

Dreo grabbed his wrist, stopping Gray's jerky movements with his steady grip. He applied gentle pressure, squeezing gradually tighter until Gray looked up, effectively trapping him in the Demon's smoldering gaze.

"Explain yourself," Dreo demanded, his tone calm yet firm.

"I don't have to explain anything to you," Gray growled. He jerked his arm, trying to break free of Dreo's grip, but found himself to be no match for the Demon's superior strength.

"Oh, yes you do," Dreo snarled, pulling Gray in tighter against his body. "You don't get to make a blanket statement like that, without any explanation. What have my people ever done to you to cause such distrust and animosity?"

"You're Demons," Gray sneered. "Your mere existence causes distrust and animosity. Your entire reason for being is to encourage others to give into sin. I'm just confused as to why you claim to need my help with this. I would assume if someone did murder your leader, you guys would be throwing them a party or something. Aren't you guys all for killing, stealing and corrupting the innocent?"

"You know nothing of a Demon's true purpose!" Dreo roared angrily, his eyes glowing red with the fire within. "Demons do not try to corrupt or harm the everyday human in hopes of claiming their souls. We tempt those with evil souls in an effort to push them over the edge, into damnation. Those souls have no place in the mortal world with regular people. Torment of the innocent would be pointless to us. It would be a tremendous amount of work, with very little benefit. Only damned souls can sustain us."

"Oh, I know plenty about a Demon's purpose," Gray responded, rage welling within him, fighting to be set free. "I've seen the aftermath with my own eyes. Tell me, Andreo Demos, what kind of evil act an eight-year-old boy could be guilty of that would put him in the sights of a Demon's version of *justice*? What could he have possibly done to deserve being beaten within an inch of his life before finally—mercifully—having his throat cut and his small, broken body discarded like yesterday's trash? Please—tell me again about your *purpose!*"

His chest heaved and his stomach rolled as Gray fought back the waves of nausea that battered him. The memory, nearly ten years past, was once again fighting its way to the surface.

A gentle breeze had been blowing, cutting through the oppressive humidity that had been plaguing the city for weeks. Gray remembered the rusty scent of blood in the air and the sound of water dripping on the ground—only it hadn't actually been water. Gray wished it had been something that mundane.

He had cut between two buildings, hurrying to make it home before the orphanage locked its doors for the night. Little had he known that the alley he found himself in wouldn't lead him home, but into a nightmare in the form of Henry Allen Fuller's bled out and brutalized body.

The one thing that had terrified his fifteen-year-old self more than the poor boy's exsanguinated corpse, had been the monster responsible for it, still hunched over the boy's prone form. Whether he had just completed the act when Gray had happened upon them, or if he had stayed to admire his work, Gray had never found out. What he did know was that no matter how long he lived, he would never be able to erase the face of the murderer, or the hellfire that had been burning in his eyes, from his mind.

It had been in that moment, faced with the aftermath of such Demonic depravity, that Gray had decided that Demons were evil beings that were beyond redemption. It was for that reason that no Demon would enjoy the advantages that came from the use of Gray's services. In his opinion, they had lost the right by allowing such a creature to roam the streets, undeterred. There had been no punishment handed out—no justice served for Henry Allen Fuller. Little by little, the world had moved on and forgotten what had been done to the poor boy. Gray, however, had never forgotten and he would never forgive. Every day he went out into the world, striving for justice in the name of a boy he had never even known.

With arms crossed over his chest, Dreo watched him in silence. The directness of his stare was unnerving and Gray fought the urge to squirm under the weight of it. He couldn't understand the effect the other man had on him. Andreo Demos' presence filled him with an odd combination of apprehension and arousal. Neither was an emotion Gray felt comfortable with in regards to the Demon.

When Dreo prowled toward him, it was all Gray could do to keep himself from backing away in answer. With the Demon's body in such close proximity, Gray's heart sped up and his body heated in response. Boxed in as he was between his desk and the approaching Demon, he knew there would be no escape for him.

"Grayson."

Dreo's voice was rough, like he had spent the night shouting out his pleasure. Gray licked his lips, his mouth gone dry at the picture that was now burned into his mind. He was shocked at how easily he was able to bring forth an image of himself, on his hands and knees, on display for the powerful Demon. Dreo's hard body mounting Gray from behind. His strong fingers digging into Gray's hips as he plowed forcefully into Gray's hungry hole, while Gray loved every second of it. Gray became so lost in the image, time no longer had meaning. It could have been seconds, or hours, later when Dreo's deep voice brought him back to reality.

"While I am truly sorry for the horror that you witnessed, to paint all Demons with that same brush is grossly unfair. Should I judge all humans by the actions of Hitler or Manson?"

Gray almost choked on his retort. While he hated fighting, what he disliked even more was when the person he was arguing with actually had a valid point. It sort of took the wind right out of his sails. He folded his arms over his chest and pinned the man with his most fearsome glare, the one that usually sent annoying detectives and nagging reporters running in the opposite direction.

Unfortunately, Andreo Demos appeared to be immune to Gray's anger. Possibly a side effect from all that time spent in hell? A wistful smile teased the corner of the man's mouth as he took one last step into Gray's personal space. The movement connected their bodies from chest to thigh and sent an electrical sensation jolting through Gray. He felt like he had stuck his finger in a light socket. His skin practically crackled everywhere they made contact. As he stared at the Demon's sinful mouth, the urge to press his lips against Dreo's, to close that final distance, was almost more than Gray could fight.

As his resolve crumbled, Gray leaned in, prepared to throw caution to the wind. A loud bang and a muffled curse sounded out from the lobby and dragged him forcefully back to reality. At the realization of what he had almost done, he jerked back, desperate to put distance between them so he could clear his head. A knowing smile curled Dreo's lips, but he, thankfully, said nothing. Slowly backing away, he allowed Gray the space he was so desperate for.

Taking a calming breath, Gray dared a glance up at his dark seductor. The man's eyes were smoldering, flames made of hellfire flickering in their dark depths. Gray was surprised to find that, in the case of Andreo Demos, the hint of hellfire that he normally found so repulsive only served to make him hotter for the man. The evidence of the Demon within and all his barely leashed power was intoxicating.

"Point taken," Gray murmured, trying to focus his attention back to their conversation. "So, what's the other part of the job?"

Dreo met his gaze, his raised brow a clear challenge that set Gray's heart pounding in his chest, but he did his best to ignore it. "The second is just a small matter of succession. For Demons, there is no clear line to the throne. Under normal circumstances, there would have been a challenge announced and a fight to determine who was the strongest and best equipped to rule. In this case, however, no legitimate challenge was declared. From all appearances, someone drugged our king and slit his throat while he slept. Therefore, whoever is responsible will be facing murder charges and will have no claim to the throne."

Gray frowned. "Didn't your king have a family or children that are old enough to take over in his place?"

Dreo shook his head, his expression somber. "It is rare for Demons to breed through natural means. We are able to create biological children if we find our destined mates. Until that time, we are completely sterile. That being said, some make the decision to sire new Demons, feeling that it is an acceptable alternative."

"You mean—turn a human into a Demon?"

"Yes, that is correct."

"I had no idea you could turn someone into a Demon. I thought that was just a vampire thing. Is it difficult?"

"It involves a ritual, Demon magic and, of course, a blood exchange. Only the oldest of us dare to attempt it. The ritual takes a great deal of power. If the Demon attempting it is not strong enough, it can burn out both the Demon and the fledgling he is trying to turn. It is dangerous at the best of times. In the wrong hands, it can be deadly. Honestly, I can't even remember the last time someone tried it."

Comprehension flared within Gray. "Wow! You guys are like the endangered species of the paranormal community. I guess it's a good thing Demons live forever, huh? Now, as to the matter of succession," Gray continued, "how do you think I'm going to be able to help with that?"

A smirk appeared at the corner of Dreo's sensual mouth. "With your powers, you are able to look into the future, at all possible outcomes, correct?"

"Yes," Gray admitted hesitantly, unsure where the Demon was heading with his line of questioning.

"Then this task should be easy for you," Dreo responded with a nod. "We need you to *See* and determine what Demon would be best to elevate to Lord of the Underworld."

Silence filled the room while he stared at Dreo. Gray's eyes flared wide, before he broke out laughing. "Oh sure," he gasped, trying to catch his breath, "easy. You're kidding, right?"

Dreo's brow furrowed. "I don't see what is so funny. Why would I be kidding?" Confusion was clear in his tone, as well as his tight-lipped expression.

Gray managed to regain control of himself and his laughter died down to an occasional hiccup. "Let me make sure I'm understanding you correctly. You want me to not only find out who is responsible for murdering the previous Lord of the Underworld, but also determine who should be next in line to over the position?"

"Yes, you understand quite well. I do not see the problem."

"Of course you don't," Gray huffed, no longer amused. "Well, thanks for the offer, but my answer is *no*." Turning away, he focused his attention back to the disaster that was his desk. That being the case, he totally missed Dreo's quick shift across the room until the Demon had him pinned to the wall with a hand around his throat. While it wasn't cutting of his air supply—yet—it did render him immobile. Surprised, Gray looked up into eyes gone black, burning with barely controlled hellfire.

"This is not a joke, Mr Muir. This is an extremely serious situation that is going to escalate rapidly if it is not resolved soon."

"I don't see how that's my problem," Gray shot back, too angry to act rationally. Grasping the other man's hand at his throat, he tried to peel away the offending fingers but found he would've had more luck trying to move solid stone. Andreo Demos wouldn't be going anywhere until he decided he was ready to go. Gray's feeble attempts for freedom did nothing to improve his situation, while earning him a dark scowl from the other man.

Dreo's answering growl resonated through Gray's body and settled in his groin, bringing his cock quickly to life. Gray desperately tried to bite back the groan that was building in his chest, but wasn't sure he was successful. The look on Dreo's face said that he wasn't doing a very good job hiding his attraction to the gorgeous Lust Demon.

Expecting his handsome captor to lash out at him again, Gray was surprised when Dreo gently cupped his jaw with his free hand. "There are many factions in the Underworld who would do almost anything to take over leadership," he responded, with a calm that belayed his previous actions. "If we cannot announce a successor soon, these factions will rise up and blood will flow in the streets. Many innocents, both human and para, will die in their bid for power. That is not something any of us wish to see happen."

"If the Demon Counsel sent you, you must be a pretty powerful guy. Why don't you step up and take the throne? Problem solved."

The laugh that resonated from Dreo was a deep, rich sound that did funny things to Gray's insides. "No, Grayson Muir. The throne is not meant for me. I can do more for my people as a free man than if I was tied to that chair. No. There are others much better suited for the responsibility that comes with being the leader of the Underworld."

Dreo continued to observe him, waiting for him to make a decision. Gray remained frozen under the power of the other man's stare, watching as the banked flames in his dark orbs swelled, once again evolving into a raging inferno of sweltering hellfire.

Leaning forward, Dreo placed a chaste kiss on the corner of Gray mouth. The action was completely at odds with the heat Gray saw building in the other man's eyes. With shock rendering him paralyzed, the lip lock was over before Gray even had a chance to react. When Dreo pulled away to meet his gaze, Gray saw the flames had died down to a steady smolder.

"We are desperate, Grayson Muir," Dreo whispered. "We need you. Will you help us?"

Gazing into those fiery eyes, Gray felt his mind fog with lust he knew had nothing to do with Dreo's powers, and everything to do with his own rampant libido. Simply put, he wanted Andreo Demos with a fierceness he'd never experienced before. Gray knew the attraction he felt was stupid. It was dangerous to have a relationship with a Demon, be it simply sexual or something more. Demons were dangerous. He understood that fact better than most.

As an Oracle, he'd witnessed much of the depravity the world had to offer, both human and paranormal alike. If he gave in to his attraction for this Demon, he would be putting more at risk than just his heart. The smartest thing to do would be to just walk away. It's not like he needed the money. His profession was in high demand and, therefore, had a very lucrative fee that reflected that fact. He was set for life. Unfortunately, people would be at risk if the situation escalated. That was something he couldn't let happen. He was willing to risk a lot to keep the innocents of the world safe, even his own soul, if it came right down to it.

Decision made, Gray leaned into the Demon's hard body, lifted his head and brushed his lips against Dreo's in a soft whisper of a kiss. He flicked out his tongue, desperate for a taste of the man holding him.

He knew he was playing with fire, but when it came to Andreo Demos, it seemed he had no control.

Dreo snagged Gray's bottom lip between his teeth, briefly, before kissing away the sting. "Does this mean you agree to help us?" he whispered against Gray's mouth.

With a final pass of his tongue over the seam of Dreo's lips, Gray pulled back and met the Demon's lust-blown glaze. The beauty of his expression was like a punch to the gut. Gray inhaled deeply, trying to force air back into his lungs.

The whole situation had 'train wreck' written all over it. That fact had him second-guessing himself. He was normally able to maintain a level of professional distance on any of the cases he took on. In order to be effective—and stay sane—a minimum degree of separation was necessary. Without it, he ran the risk of letting his emotions lead his *Sight*, which increased the chance of inaccurate visions. It also raised the risk that he might not be able to *See* anything at all. His lust for Dreo had his emotions running at an all-time high and he had never been one for letting his dick do the thinking for him. Besides, Dreo was a Demon. Gray still wasn't convinced the man was on the level. For all he knew, Dreo could be a homicidal Demon, hell-bent on Gray's torture and ultimate destruction.

Gray took a breath and gave Dreo the only answer he had.

"Let me think about it."

Chapter Three

Thursday morning had Gray back in his office, wrapping up a consultation. It had been three days since Dreo had stormed out of his office. The man had made it abundantly clear that Gray's answer to his request for help was unsatisfactory. After growling out what he was sure were some choice Demonic curses, Dreo had kissed him within an inch of his life before demanding Gray contact him once he had made his decision. The Demon had then slammed a business card down on his desk before vanishing from the room without a trace. Gray would have believed the whole confrontation had been a product of an overactive imagination and sleep deprivation if it hadn't been for the subtle scent of sulfur lingering in the air and that damn business card that had been taunting him from the corner of his desk.

He had spent the last few days jumping at shadows, half expecting the man to just appear and demand his compliance. Every time a tall, dark haired man walked by, he caught himself looking to see if it was the gorgeous Demon. The disappointment he felt when the Demon didn't show was definitely something he hadn't expected. While he was still convinced that getting involved with Andreo Demos would be the worst decision he'd ever made—even worse than the time he'd agreed to let his elderly neighbor lady set him up on a blind date with her grandson, who'd ended up having a strange obsession with ingesting tin foil—he could admit that there was something about the other man that intrigued him to the point of distraction.

Ridiculously, Gray had been under the mistaken impression that Dreo returned his feelings. The last few days of silence, however, had put the kibosh on that line of thinking. Gray berated himself for his foolishness. He was never one to fall so quickly. His track record with relationships was shit. Because of that, he'd learned to always be cautious when entering into a new relationship. From men who were caught up in the allure of being with an Oracle, to the plain old everyday crazies, it was hard for Gray to let down his guard. Getting involved with a Demon would be a guaranteed broken heart. It was best to clear his head of all things Demon and focus on what was important—his work.

His meeting that morning was with the CEO of a major engineering company. Some might think that was strange, but people came to him from all walks of life, seeking all kinds of information. Anything from who they should marry, to whether or not it would be a bad idea to start mass marketing nuclear weapons. He had heard it all. Thankfully, this client's needs were much more mundane. The middle-aged business man just needed insight into the best direction to take his company for future growth and profitability.

It was Gray's policy to never dole out advice for people to follow. In his opinion, that was a completely different line of work, one he had no desire to delve into. All he did was see possible futures. Who was he to decide what the best one was? It was Gray's belief that it was his job to present the options. When faced with all the possible outcomes, most people were able to choose the best course of action on their own. Very rarely did it become a matter of trying to choose the lesser evil. In those cases, he had a psychiatrist, an Empath, a life coach, an accountant and a private detective that he referred people to, depending on their need. He was only equipped to deal with *Seeing* — everything else, he left to the professionals.

He wrapped up his client consultation quickly. It was a straightforward request and would take just one sitting to get the information the man desired. Gray led him to the lobby, where Sarah would get him set up with his appointment.

As he rounded the corner, he caught a whiff of sulfur a moment before he registered a familiar figure looming in the corner of the lobby. His heartbeat picked up to a frantic pace, despite his efforts to remain indifferent to his presence. The man was gorgeous. Dressed in dark denim, a black T-shirt, and a steel gray military jacket, Dreo still managed to look regal and imposing. His long fall of hair had been pulled back into a queue, allowing Gray to be hit with the full power of those amazing eyes. He nearly gasped aloud at the raw need he saw reflected there. Gray had hoped the Demon's effect on him during their last meeting had been a fluke, never to be repeated. It was clear that was not the case.

Doing his best to ignore the man, Gray walked his client over to Sarah, giving his assistant a brief explanation of what they needed to have set up. With their appointment finalized, Gray bid the gentleman farewell before turning his attention back to what he was now considering 'his Demon'.

"How can I help you today, Mr Demos?" The words were polite and professional. His suggestive tone was anything but. Gray drank in the sight of the tall Demon as he fought back the urge to climb his body like a tree. Man, did he want another taste of that.

"There are many ways you can help me, Grayson Muir, but for now, we will settle for the matter of you taking on my case and discovering who killed our Lord. I have allowed you more than enough time to consider the matter," Dreo stated firmly. "I need your answer. If I cannot secure your assistance, we will need to look into other means of resolving the situation."

Gray frowned. "When we spoke before, you insinuated that I was your only option to fix the problem. Now, you seem to be brimming with solutions. What's changed?"

Crossing his thick arms over his chest, Dreo scowled down at Gray. "I never said that you were our only solution, just the best one. We have other means of flushing out the perpetrator, however, they wouldn't be as tactful as having you discover the truth." Dreo shrugged, dismissively. "In lieu of other alternatives, we can always declare a hunt for the guilty party. Eventually, he or she will be brought to justice, but innocents may be harmed in the process. Utilizing your gifts would help us minimize the reality of unwanted violence."

Dreo's expression was fierce, further inciting the hunger building inside Gray. He was consumed with thoughts of his Demon stripping him bare and mounting him in the office lobby, without a care to may see their coupling. It was disconcerting to say the least. While Dreo's expression was all business, Gray could see the barely contained fire in Dreo's eyes. He wasn't as unaffected as he might like to appear. Gray smirked, a sense of victory filling him.

"Sarah! How's the rest of my day looking?" He threw a look over his shoulder, smiling in the face of her scowl. She really hated when he shouted for her.

"You're clear for the rest of the weekend," she announced a few key strokes later. "You don't have another appointment until Monday afternoon." Her smug expression made Gray want to pinch her. She knew he wasn't happy about this job. He'd been hoping she would be a good friend and give him an out. Glowering at her lack of loyalty, he received a finger wave in response. Giving her up as a lost cause, he turned back to the sexy Demon who was staring at him expectantly.

"Fine!" Exasperated, he grabbed his jacket off the stand by the door. "If you need anything, I'll probably be unreachable. Hell gets terrible cell service."

Sarah laughed. "I'm sure I can hold the fort for a few days without anything catastrophic happening. You boys have fun."

"Yeah, that's real great advice for someone taking a trip to the Underworld," Gray grumbled. He left the office with the sound of Sarah's laughter still ringing in his ears and a feeling of foreboding burning in his stomach. Hell was a dangerous place at the best of times. Heading there in hopes of flushing out a killer was a death wish in the making. Gray hoped that any death involved with their trip wouldn't be his own.

* * * *

Travel to Hell was surprisingly easy, a fact that Gray was extremely grateful for. All it took was a bit of privacy and a few muttered words from Dreo and, before he knew it, they were standing in a marbled courtyard under a hazy black sky. It only took a moment for a wave of sticky heat to settle over them, practically suffocating Gray with its weight. Gray was grateful he had dressed in light clothes and left his jacket at home, as moisture was already beading on his skin. He struggled at first, gasping and choking for air. It was similar to trying to inhale in a sauna, magnified by a thousand. Taking a few deep gulps, he sighed in relief when he eventually settled back into a normal breathing pattern.

No longer in danger of asphyxiating, Gray allowed himself a moment to take in his surroundings. At a glance, the Underworld didn't appear that different from a normal human town. Homes and storefronts lined the streets and littered the landscape. Men, women and children wandered freely, running errands and just going about their lives. Everything was just so…normal. It was almost too easy to forget the fact that this wasn't a regular neighborhood and these weren't ordinary people. Any doubts he had about that were quashed when an explosion sounded, shaking the ground and rattling windows. Instantly alert, Gray focused on finding the location of the disruption.

Trusting his senses, Gray turned his gaze toward the outskirts of the civilized little mecca. When the glowing flames of the Pits came into view, there was no doubt in Gray's mind that they were the source of the disturbance. They sparked and hissed as hellfire broke through the cracked earth, erupting in fountains of molten flame. It would have been a beautiful sight if Gray didn't know the true purpose of the Pits. Even as the thought crossed his mind, he could swear he could hear the echo of screams in the distance.

Raised voices sounded off to his left, tearing his focus away from the landscape. Turning his attention to the disruption, Gray's eye caught on two Demon males locked together in some kind of altercation. Shouts and curses fell from their mouths as a feeling of unease swashed over Gray. He was about to say something to Dreo when one of the men roared and sent a ball of blue flame hurtling toward the other man. In a move almost faster than Gray's eyes could track, the other Demon threw himself to the side, just managing to miss being barbequed alive, as the fireball crashed into a vacant storefront. As it was, the smell of scorched hair filled the air. The downed man pulled himself to his feet, his expression a mask of rage. The man's hands erupted into yellow flames as he bore down on his attacker. Casting a worried glance up at Dreo, Gray was surprised to see nothing more than irritation coloring his face.

"Don't you think you should stop them?" The sound of another fireball making contact with a building had Gray cringing.

"There is little point," Dreo said dismissively. "This is only the beginning of the chaos that will ensue if we cannot find the guilty party soon. The Demon Council has been forced to put up wards to keep the Underworld on lockdown since Lucifer was found dead. It is impossible for anyone to come or go without approval from the Council. While some Demons are happy living so close to others of our kind, there are others who prefer seclusion. Forcing so many Demons to be in such close proximity for any period of time is like lighting a stick of dynamite and waiting for it to explode. It is inevitable. Our only hope is that we can resolve the situation before too much damage is done." Turning away from the fight, Dreo motioned for him to follow.

Gray swallowed nervously, trailing Dreo. Nothing like working under pressure. They quickly made their way through the bustling streets until they found themselves standing before the large iron gates of Lord Lucifer's palace. Dreo shared a few quietly whispered words with the demons guarding the entrance before they were ushered in with no further delay.

Gray couldn't help but marvel at the dark splendor of their surroundings. The black marble that covered the floors was shot through with veins of silver, turquoise and violet. That, combined with deep royal-blue walls, gave the appearance that the entire palace was cast in a constant state of twilight. The beauty and peace emanating from their surroundings was in complete opposition to what Gray had been expecting to find in Hell. Sculptures and tapestries lined the walls as they passed, depicting everything from fallen rulers to events from times long past. Gray was tempted to stop for a closer look but decided against it. Instead, he tried to keep pace with Dreo, who was moving at a steady clip toward what he had described as the main receiving hall. It was there that they were supposed to meet up with Dreo's team of demons who would be acting as Gray's protection during his investigation. Guards were dispersed along the way, cleverly hidden in the shadows of the majestic sculptures. They remained motionless as he and Dreo passed, but Gray wasn't fooled. He could see the tension in their bodies and the sharpness of their stares. They were ready to move into action at the slightest sign of trouble. Gray could admit he was adequately impressed.

Passing through a massive stone archway, Gray found himself entering a beautifully decorated throne room. The cavernous space was well over the length of a football field and decorated in the same style as the rest of the castle he'd seen. Crystal chandeliers hung from the ceiling, dripping with pale purple and silver gems that cast an enchanting glow over the room. Black doors lined the walls of the hall, leading the way deeper into the castle. What Gray wouldn't give to have free reign to explore the gigantic structure. Who knew what lay beyond those doors? The endless possibilities teased at his inherent tendency toward curiosity. He gave them one last wistful glance before following after Dreo's retreating form.

Continuing on, Gray finally noticed the Demons milling around the room. Dressed to the nines, they were clearly from the higher echelon of Demon society. Dreo paid them no mind as he continued through the throng, clearing a path with nothing more than his presence. Gray tried to emulate Dreo's dismissive attitude as he walked at his side. It became more and more difficult as he found himself on the receiving end of some interested glances. Some were merely curious, while others were downright hostile. Shrugging it off, Gray reminded himself that he wasn't here to make friends. He had a job to do and when it was complete, he would never see these people again.

They were nearly halfway across the hall when they were intercepted by a small contingent of soldiers. Half a dozen men seemed to appear out of nowhere.

Battle ready, they quickly moved to surround Dreo and Gray. Gray had no idea what was happening and answers didn't appear to be forthcoming. The expression on Dreo's face left Gray reluctant to ask any questions about their, less than, warm welcome.

"What is the meaning of this?" Dreo's eyes were blazing with barely leashed hellfire. Whatever the reason, Andreo Demos was pissed. The soldiers, seemingly oblivious to his mounting fury, held their positions. A large, barrel-chested man stepped forward, a sneer plastered on his ruddy face.

"Povell." Dreo gave the man a nod of acknowledgment before pinning him with an expectant glare.

"My apologies, Andreo. We—"

"Lord Demos." Dreo's interruption was firm and immediate—his authority unquestionable.

"Excuse me?"

Povell's face was a mask of confusion. Gray had to admit, he wasn't sure why the interruption had been necessary. Maybe Dreo suffered from some form of Tourette's?

Dreo's dark brow furrowed. "You take liberties that are not yours for the taking. You will address me by my title, Povell, as my station demands." His tone brooked no argument.

Povell took a shuddering breath as his eyes widened at Dreo's harsh tone. He looked as if someone had struck him. The expression he directed at Dreo was filled with such shock and longing, it was easy to see that there was history between them. If he'd had any doubt, the vision that followed moments later, of Dreo and Povell playing mattress mambo, served as confirmation of what he had already suspected. While the vision acknowledged the reality that they had once been bed mates, it also reinforced the fact that theirs was not a true love connection. At least not for Dreo, in any case. Any claims of love or deeper affection had been absolutely one sided.

Gray felt a moment of pity for the other man. As someone who had found himself in a similar situation in the past, he understood the devastation that came with such complete rejection by an ex-lover. Feeling the need to comfort the other man, Gray took a step forward but was stopped in his tracks by the hard, venomous glare Povell aimed in his direction.

"Who the fuck are you?" The sharpness of his voice and the steely glint in his eyes had Gray feeling like a bug under a microscope. Apparently, the man had reasoned that Gray was competition for Dreo's affections. From the demon's pinched, angry expression, it was clear that he and Povell were not destined to be friends. The scowl he leveled on Gray further cemented the fact that the man wished Gray a very slow and extremely painful death.

Not one to get caught up in other people's drama, Gray yawned in the face of Povell's jealousy. He'd forgotten how exhausting people and their trivial issues could be. As someone who saw the worst the world had to offer on a daily basis, he didn't have the time or energy to deal with things like petty jealousy. He preferred to direct his focus to areas where he could make a difference. Dealing with the drama queen ex, of some guy who wasn't even his boyfriend, didn't even make it on his list.

Stepping forward, Gray held out his hand in greeting. "I'm Grayson Muir. Lord Demos has hired me as a consultant. He's asked me to look into the death of your king."

"Oh, that—right." Povell laughed derisively. "The fortune teller."

"Oracle, actually." Gray smirked at the attempted jibe. "I understand your confusion. It can sometimes be difficult for paras with a lower power base to tell the difference between the two. Don't worry," Gray said sweetly. "No harm, no foul."

"Excuse me?" Povell snarled, his eyes flashing with anger.

"It's nothing to be ashamed of," Gray continued sympathetically. "Some paras just don't possess enough magic to distinguish the difference between humans, paras and mystics. Don't let it get you down."

"You little shit!" Povell roared, taking a menacing step toward Gray. Before he could complete his move, Dreo had a strong grip on his shoulder and shoved him back, not allowing him to gain even an inch.

"Because of our past friendship, I will let you walk away with a warning just his one time—do not touch Grayson Muir. He is an honored guest and is here at my request. Any harm that befalls him, I will take as a personal attack on myself and will treat it as such. Trust me when I tell you that you do not want to know how I handle those who seek to strike out at me."

Povell turned his attention back to Dreo, his full mouth twisted into a sneering mockery of a smile. "My apologies—Lord Demos. If you would come with us, I have orders from the Council to detain you, and anyone in your company. You are wanted for questioning in regards to the death of Lord Lucifer." Despite the man's contrite words, it easy to see that he was barely able to contain his enjoyment with their current situation.

"You are making a mistake, Povell." Dreo's tone was stern, dripping with disapproval.

"No, *Lord Demos*. You are the one who made a mistake. I am doing my duty and following orders. You'd know all about that," he sneered. "If I'm remembering correctly, duty to your position and duty to your race have always been first and foremost in your heart. Or, perhaps your new choice in company has left you confused about where your loyalties lie?" Povell's expression was neutral, but his eyes were filled with an unspoken challenge that immediately put Gray on edge.

"Now is not the time to bring up old grievances," Dreo chastised. "It hardly matters now, almost a century after the fact."

"It hardly mattered then," Povell countered, his words tinged with anger and old pain. "Trust me, you made that more than clear."

Dreo's expression softened, taking a step toward his ex-lover. "I'm sorry, old friend. I admit, my thoughts and actions back then were careless. I never intended to hurt you."

Povell jerked, the words connecting like a physical blow. Brows pulled down, his eyes narrowed as he focused dark look on Dreo. "Intended or not, the past cannot be undone. We all have to live with our own choices and their consequences, both the good and the bad."

Povell was pushing Dreo's buttons, looking for a fight. If he wasn't careful, he was going to get more than he bargained for. Gray could sense the rage and regret warring behind Dreo's calm exterior. There was no telling what could happen if he allowed that anger free reign.

Watching Povell warily, Gray felt a slight change in the air, followed by a prickle behind his eyes. His vision began to dim, becoming hazy around the edges. *Damn it! Not now!*

For the most part, Gray had control of his gift, choosing when or if he would *See*. In some cases, however, the Oracle blood within him was able to sense a wrongness or need, and would drag him into a vision, whether he wanted to *See* or not. Gray hated the loss of control, but he hated what he was usually forced to witness, more. A spontaneous vision was never filled with sunshine and roses. Whenever he was forced to *See*, it was usually to bring light to an unmentionable wrong. Something that needed to be stopped immediately. With his ability sparking to life, Gray knew he was about to be on the receiving end of nightmare. He also knew he didn't want to have to face it alone.

He grabbed Dreo's arm, needing the other man's attention. When the Demon met his gaze, Gray was surprised by the concern he saw reflected there. Shaking off his shock, he knew he only had moments to act before he was pulled into his other sight.

"Would you like the chance to see through the eyes of an Oracle, *Lord Demos*?"

Normally, Gray would never offer to allow someone else to hitch a ride on one of his visions. In many cases, the things he saw were of the worst humanity had to offer — murder, kidnapping, abuse — just for a start. He would never chose to subject someone else with that kind of horror, just for the novelty of it. It served only to trivialize his gift. Unfortunately, this situation was different. Something within him told him that this one was going to be bad, and Dreo needed to see it.

Picking up on the urgency of the situation, Dreo didn't hesitate to nod his consent. Taking the other man's hand in a firm grip, Gray turned to fully meet his eyes. He saw confusion and concern but, thankfully, no fear. At least, not yet.

"What do I do?" Dreo questioned, nervousness just a small gleam in his eyes.

Gray smiled gently. "Just focus on me. The rest will happen on its own." He didn't tell Dreo that he could already feel the images building up, just waiting for admittance into his mind. The oily feel and the shiver up his spine confirmed his earlier suspicion. This one was going to be a bad. As his vision dimmed to black, he gave Dreo's hand one last firm squeeze. "No matter what you see, remember that you are safe, okay?"

"I don't understand."

"You will," Gray said, sadly. "Forgive me."

Chapter Four

The vision played out before them, like clips from a horror movie. It didn't take long for Gray to realize why these events needed to be seen. Scene after scene flashed before his eyes.

Povell beating a female Demon with a spiked chain as she hunched protectively over a small Demon child. Povell slitting the throat of a battered human man as he cowered and begged for his life. Povell and another Demon abducting young men and women, violating them in ways Gray couldn't have imagined in his worst nightmare –

On and on, the images flashed before them, each new scene worse than the last. Gray's stomach began to churn. The horror of what they were being forced to bear witness to was just too much. In his line of work, he had seen some truly horrific things, but he'd never seen anything close to this level of depravity. As he struggled to push down the growing urge to lose his lunch, he felt the swelling tide of Dreo's rage brush against him and sizzle against his skin. It was oddly comforting to know that he was not alone in this nightmare. Even when enraged, Dreo's presence soothed him. A full body tremor worked its way through Gray, leaving him a wrung out, nauseated mess. As his normal sight started to return, he couldn't remember ever being more grateful to return to reality.

As soon as his vision cleared, Gray's stomach gave a vicious twist and he was moving. He shoved his way through the surrounding guards and Demons, desperately trying to get clear of the teeming masses. He made one last push, finally managing to get clear of the crowd, before losing the contents of his stomach in a nearby corner. Hunched over and heaving, he was startled by the heavy weight of a hand coming down to rest on his back. His tension vanished when he recognized Dreo's familiar presence. He fought back a moan as the other man began rubbing his back in soothing circles.

"Are you all right?" Even the harshness of his tone did nothing to mask the concern Gray heard in Dreo's words.

Glancing over his shoulder at the room full of people, Gray's face burned with embarrassment. He usually had a much stronger stomach. Dragging himself to his feet, he wiped his mouth with the back of his hand. Straightening his shirt, he met the other man's gaze with barely leashed anger. "I'm fine. What are you standing around for? We've got work to do."

Respect warmed Dreo's gaze, clearing away the worry. "As you say."

With a sharp nod to Gray, Dreo turned back to the assembled crowd that seemed to get grow with every passing minute. As he started forward, the crowd parted before him. Gray imagined it had something do to with the expression on Dreo's face. That kind of malevolent rage, coupled with the power of a high level Demon, was enough to scare even the bravest of Demons.

Coming to stand before Povell, Dreo stared at the other man in contempt. "To think, I once considered you an honored friend. You have always held a place in my heart, just as you once held a place in my bed. Your compassion and kindness, your strength and bravery. They made you a good man...a respected man. While love between us was never in the cards, our friendship would have lived on forever. You have betrayed your people and your purpose with your actions. Did you honestly think you would be able to continue this way and never be caught? You are an abomination!"

Turning his attention to the guards, he scanned the surrounding Demons. "Balen!" A large, blond Demon separated himself from the crowd. He made his approach without fear, a cocky grin on his lips.

"Master Demos," the Demon, Balen, greeted with a dip of his head. "How may I be of service?"

"Take Povell into custody."

"The charges?" Balen asked curiously.

"Assault, kidnapping, rape, torture, murder, genocide and treason. There may be more charges added later, after the full investigation is underway."

As gasps and frantic whispers sounded through the crowd, Dreo glared at Povell, daring him to dispute the charges. The man, who just moments earlier had been filled with superiority and malice, seemed to shrink under the weight of Dreo's stare. His shoulders hunched and he began to tremble violently.

"Andreo," Povell gasped. "You can't do this. Our friendship has spanned centuries. How can you believe anything he showed you more than my own word?"

"Because he is *The Oracle!*" Dreo growled. "The prophecies have been proven true in him. He sees the truth in all things — past, present and future. His knowledge is absolute. I have witnessed it with my own eyes."

The truth in Dreo's words rang ominously through the hall and suddenly, Gray felt very afraid. He'd been prepared to be part of a discreet investigation. He had agreed to *See* the death of the previous Lord, identify the murderer then go back to business as usual. An announcement like the one Dreo had just made was not designed with discretion in mind, nor would it go unanswered. As it stood, he already had enough people who would like to kill him for the things he had *Seen*. He knew nothing about the prophecies Dreo spoke of and was pretty sure he didn't want to. He had plenty of pressure serving the clients he had, as well as the work he did for the police. With prophecies, there was always the involvement of a higher power, destiny and enormous expectations. Gray couldn't handle any more responsibilities. He was maxed out already. As far as Gray was concerned, his only destiny was to protect his 'family' and to look out for those who came to him for help. Anything past that was beyond his ability to handle. If Dreo thought he could force something like this on him, then it was definitely time for him to leave.

Turning away, Gray scanned the room, looking for the quickest exit. Noticing a break in the crowd, he had just made a step toward freedom, when a hand came down on his shoulder, stopping him in tracks.

"Don't even think about it, Oracle."

Gray flinched at the warning in Dreo's words. He was a mess of mixed emotions as the sound of the Demon's deep, rumbling voice worked its way through him. While logic told him it would be smartest to run for the hills, his body craved the comfort of Dreo's touch with a need unlike anything he had ever felt before. Besides Sarah, Gray had never had anyone in his life who'd cared for him as a person, more than they cared about him being an Oracle. Even Stephen, who had rode to his rescue during his darkest hour, tended to focus mainly on the part of him that was Oracle, and ignored anything else. Gray knew that his friend didn't do it on purpose. Because of his own self-sufficiency, people tended to assume that nothing fazed him and Gray allowed them to believe the lie. It seemed too much like a weakness to admit that sometimes, after a really bad day, he would give anything to just have someone hold him and tell him that everything was going to be all right. As he looked up into Dreo's eyes, he felt a glimmer of hope spark within him. Maybe—just maybe—this was man who could hold him together when his world was falling apart. Maybe Dreo could be the man that Gray told all of his secrets to, both good and bad, and still loved him despite them. Because of the nature of their gift, Oracles didn't tend to keep lovers long. Gray had never dared to dream that he would find someone who could truly be his other half. He couldn't help himself from hoping that Dreo could possibly be that man.

The pull to be near him was more than Gray was able to fight. He leaned in, plastering his body against Dreo's. The new proximity allowed him to feel every dip, ridge and swollen inch of the sinfully gorgeous Demon. The feel of his skin was electric. Suddenly, the touch that had been designed to comfort and calm and turned into something more. It ignited a heat within Gray that he could barely understand, let alone try to control. If they hadn't been in a room full of curious onlookers, he wouldn't have hesitated to grind his growing arousal against Dreo's heavy thigh. Fortunately—or unfortunately depending on one's point of view—they were in a room full of people, and Gray had never been known to have any exhibitionist tendencies. The low, rumbling growl that sounded from the stunning man almost had him second guessing his stance on that. The sound was like a bolt of lightning to his system. Thankfully, his common sense chose that moment to kick in, beating back the lust that was trying to blind him to the reality of his situation, and awakening an anger that burned in his stomach like acid.

"Get your hand off of me, Demon," Gray snarled quietly, not wanting to make a scene with so many witnesses. He wasn't sure who he was angrier with—Dreo, for using Demonic powers on him, or himself, for letting down his guard and allowing himself to be turned into the Demon's bitch. For the moment, he'd settle on Dreo. He could beat himself up about his bad choices in men later, when his life wasn't hanging in the balance.

Shaking off Dreo's grip, he rounded on the seemingly stunned Demon. "What the fuck do you think you're doing, using your powers on me? I thought you were different. Stupidly, I thought that maybe you were beginning to care for me. I came here to do a job for you, not to audition to be the next member of your harem. Now, keep your bullshit stories and Demonic pheromones to yourself and let me work, so I can get the fuck out of here!"

Dreo stared at him, silently, for what seemed like an eternity. When Gray moved to push past him, Dreo's hand shot out, his firm grip digging into Gray's bicep.

A quick tug had him flush against the demon's massive body. Layers of rippling muscle and Dreo's gothic good looks had Gray's mouth watering. Swallowing hard to keep himself from drooling all over the sexy Demon's shirt, he looked up into eyes glowing with molten flame. It surprised him how something that should fill him with fear, instead, had him practically panting with need. Wrapping his bigger body over Gray from behind, Dreo cocooned him away from the curious eyes around them. Hot breath tickled his neck as Dreo nipped and kissed his way up his throat and across his jaw,

"For a man who *Sees* everything, you are blind to what's right in front of you. To think," he scoffed, "you would accuse me of using my powers against you?" Dreo gave Gray a pitying look. "Even if I wanted to, it would be impossible for me to use my powers on my own mate." Pushing himself away from Gray, Dreo turned back to the guards, shouting out orders and arranging transportation for the prisoner.

For the first time in his life, Gray found himself speechless. As an Oracle, he was always the first to know everything. It was rare for him to find himself in a situation where he didn't already know every possible outcome. The only true blind spots he'd ever found in his gift seemed to be if he tried to look for knowledge that directly influenced his own life. While the Fates had no problem saddling him with the 'gift' of knowing all there was to know about everyone else, he wasn't able to use it for any kind of personal gain. At first, he'd been bothered by the double standard. Now, he didn't even bother trying to look. The knowledge that he had been caught so completely unaware was both exciting and terrifying. *What could it mean?*

Raised voices caught his attention and brought his focus back to what was happening around him. Two guards had moved forward and were closing in on Povell. Heavy chains were hanging from their hands, ready to restrain the man. The murderous Demon didn't seem to be onboard with their plans. Waiting until they were within striking distance, Povell lurched forward, throwing his weight into the body of one of the approaching guards. Unthinking, the guard dropped the chains and raised his arms in an attempt stop his fall. Gray had a moment to take in the look of malicious victory on Povell's face before everything around them burst into chaos.

There was no chance to even call out a warning before Povell's hands erupted into sickly, green flame. Their glow was reflected in Povell's eyes, further accentuating the malevolent gleam in his narrowed orbs.

"Povell," Dreo placated coolly, taking a cautious step forward. "Extinguish the flames. Do not make the situation worse for yourself by causing more damage."

"Fuck you, *Lord Demos!*" Povell screamed. "You would take the word of that piece-of-shit human over me? Over your own kind? You would make yourself a traitor to your own people, all for him?" Disgust colored his expression, from his narrowed eyes to the sneer that twisted his lips.

"The only traitor to our people is you, Povell. The crimes you have committed against humans and Demons alike are beyond belief. There is a sickness in you. Something vile and festering, corrupting everything you touch. A sentence of death would be too merciful a judgment for the crimes you have committed. The Oracle has shown me the truth of your crimes. The joy you took in them. There is no arguing with what he has *Seen*."

Dreo's eyes were cold like black pieces of ice as he glared at the man before him. If he had ever felt anything for the other Demon, be it friendship or love, there was no longer any trace of it. His stony glare was hollow, empty of anything but disgust. Gray hoped that Dreo never looked at him with such disdain. Povell would not find an ally in Dreo and the man knew it.

Desperation morphed into rage. "I might not be able to argue with what the Oracle has shown you," Povell sneered, "but I can make sure it's the last things he *Sees*."

In a move faster than Gray could have ever imagined, Povell jerked his arm to the side. His flaming hands now aimed straight at Gray's face. With a final sneer and without one bit of hesitation, he appeared to relax his grip and shot a stream of fire directly at Gray, engulfing him in deadly green flame.

Chapter Five

It happened so fast, Gray didn't even have time to flinch as the burning projectile closed the space between them. The room seemed frozen. The only sound was the crackling hiss from the fire as it drew nearer. To Gray, even time itself seemed to have stopped in its tracks. What seemed like an eternity could, truly, only have been seconds then the room erupted in a flurry of noise and movement.

Screams and shouts filled the hall as the guards converged on Povell. Thankfully, there was a Water Demon present who stepped forward to lend a hand. Never having had the chance to work with one before, Gray found himself entranced by her appearance. The statuesque beauty was nearly as tall as Dreo, with long, shimmering blue hair and pale gray skin. Winding up, like a pitcher on the mound, she hammered Povell with thick silver streams of water, over and over again, until he could no longer withstand their power and was driven to his knees.

Once he was on the ground, the Water Demon really kicked it up a notch. Holding both arms out in front of her, she approached Povell's downed form, blasting him with an unending torrent of water. Between the determined glint in her eyes and the heavy fall of her hair swirling around her, she looked like an avenging angel. With a flick of her wrists, the liquid churned and rose until it became a ball of solid water, encasing Povell's body. The flames coating his hands flickered briefly before winking out of existence as their master was completely submerged in water. She continued to restrain him there until his struggling ceased and his body went limp. With the threat now neutralized, she released her hold on the water and allowed Povell's unconscious form to drop to the floor in a sopping wet heap.

Instantly, Dreo was in Gray's face, grasping his shoulders in an iron grip. His wide eyes were filled with concern as he ran hands down Gray's body, frantically searching him from head to toe for injury. Worry was quickly replaced with confusion when all he uncovered was pale, unmarred skin. There wasn't a burn or scorch mark anywhere to be found on Gray.

"How?" Dreo gasped, his brows pulled down in bafflement.

Gray shrugged sheepishly. "It kind of comes with the gig. Being an Oracle has the added benefit of a certain level of indestructability. It definitely comes in handy. As you can see," he continued, motioning to an extremely soggy Povell, who was now screaming and thrashing on the floor like a fish out of water, "people aren't always please about what I *See*."

"You're indestructible." Dreo's softly spoken words were hesitant, yet filled with wonder.

Gray shook his head. "Not completely. While I'm locked in my *Sight*, all my shields come down. In that moment, I'm vulnerable to attack."

Dreo scowled. "But you have others there to protect you during that time…"

"When I'm working for a private client, usually not. However, when I'm working in the field for the police, then definitely, yes. I have a whole team of bodyguards there to watch my back, in case things get out of hand. Unfortunately, I don't always have control over my *Sight*." Gray grimaced. "Sometimes, like today, I'm pulled into a vision and there's no stopping it. When that happens, I'm basically just dragged along for the ride. Thankfully, it doesn't happen often. If it does, the situation is always dire and in need of immediate attention."

"You have human guards?" Dreo scoffed, in derision. "Never again! From now on, you go nowhere alone. If I'm not with you, I will arrange to have Demon guards there to protect you."

Gray bristled at Dreo's highhanded command. He considered correcting the Demon's faulty assumption but decided against it. It would be more entertaining to let Dreo be surprised. It was nothing less than he deserved for being such a domineering ass.

"Whatever," Gray dismissed, with a wave of his hand. "I trust my guards and I'm not replacing them. They're like family. If you want to waste your money, go ahead and hire more guards. That's your business and I can't stop you. Now," he said, pushing away from Dreo, "since we've wrapped up the drama portion of the evening, can we get back to the job you hired me for? We still have a murderer to find."

Jerking back, Dreo looked at him in confusion. "I assumed, with Povell in custody, we already had our killer."

"Well, you assumed wrong," Gray snapped irritably. "You went through the vision with me. Did you, at any point, see Povell plot and execute the murder of the Lord of the Underworld?" When Gray received no immediate answer, he shook his head. "While Povell is one sick puppy and guilty of things I never want to see again, he did not kill your king. It seems like you've got more than one murderer roaming your halls." Crossing his arms over his chest, he smirked at Dreo. "Still sure it would be safer for me to have some Demon guards?"

"You're kind of a cocky shit, you know that?" Dreo growled.

Gray sighed dramatically. "We all have our crosses to bear." Turning his back on Dreo, he looked around at the gathered crowd. "Now, does someone have a phone I can use? Sadly, my phone plan doesn't provide coverage in the Underworld and I need to make a call."

Dreo sighed, irritation clear in his tone. "Why do you need a phone?"

"Isn't it obvious? With the state of things down here, there is no way I'm going to be able to *See* without my team with me."

"I already told you that I would arrange to have a team of guards for you," Dreo scowled. "There is no need to bring humans into the Underworld."

Gray scoffed. "You honestly think I'm going to trust any of your Demon guards more than my own men?"

"My men are absolutely trustworthy and I do not appreciate your insinuations to the contrary."

"Oh, yeah?" Gray asked, quirking a brow. "After everything that's happened, just in the last few minutes, you really want to stick with the story that all of your Demons are fine, upstanding citizens that wouldn't even hurt a fly?"

If looks could kill, the glare Dreo shot in his direction would have had him dropping dead on the spot. Thankfully, despite his obvious frustration, Dreo didn't refute his argument. After all, the evidence had been stacking up in Gray's favor ever since they had gotten to the Underworld. After everything he had seen, Gray was definitely not buying the 'gentle as a kitten' spin they were trying to attach to Demons. While he was prepared to reserve judgment before labeling them all as the ravenous, soul stealing monsters he had originally believed them to be, they were also far from being docile little lambs. To believe otherwise would be a mistake.

With a hand on his hip, Gray cocked his head and stared at Dreo expectantly. "Phone, please?"

Dreo groaned before retrieving a sleek, silver cell from his pocket and placing it gently in Gray's open palm. "As you wish, Oracle." Dreo's expression softened before he turned and made his way back over to the guards who were preparing Povell for transport. The Water Demon, it seemed, would be making the trip as a temporary guard to ensure there was no more excitement.

For a moment, Gray just stood back and observed Dreo. He found himself entranced by the play of muscles across Dreo's back and shoulders that flexed and bunched as the man moved. He had a fluidity to his movements that was surprisingly graceful for someone of his size. Gray's body began to heat as his thoughts, once again, turned away from the business at hand and more toward Dreo and himself getting down to business between the Demon's sheets.

He was so totally lost in his imagination that when a door slammed shut across the room, Gray swore he almost had a heart attack. He let out a relieved breath as he saw that it was just additional guards that were making their way over to join the growing crowd on the other side of the hall. Shaking his head, he tried to clear his thoughts. He didn't know if it was a side effect of being in the Underworld, but something was not right with him. He'd felt out of control since he'd arrived. With his brand of power, control was something he had to strictly maintain or risk falling back into the chaos that had tormented him in his youth. If he hadn't been on a job he would have taken the time to figure out what was going on with him. Unfortunately, their investigation was time sensitive and every minute longer it took to find the murderer was a minute closer the Underworld came to falling into complete pandemonium. His issues would just have to wait.

"I've gotta call Sarah," he muttered, trying to calm his racing heart.

Gray walked to the edge of the room and surveyed for danger one last time before placing the call. Luck was on his side when it immediately rang through, with only a few cracks and pops for his trouble. There were two rings then Sarah's soothing voice filled the line.

"Hello, sunshine."

Gray laughed at the endearment. "How did you know it was me?"

"Are you kidding? The call rang through with a six-six-six area code. Since I don't make a habit of rubbing elbows with the damned, I went with the easy money and assumed it was you. So, how are things down under?"

"Busy. I'm definitely gonna be earning my paycheck on this one. Things are a bit more complicated than we originally, thought. I'm going to need you to pull together a team for me."

"Are you okay?" Sarah's jovial tone disappeared in an instant and worry filled her words.

"Of, course," Gray soothed. "I've got a Demon watching my back, after all. I would just feel better with a bit of backup until we get everything sorted out." He kept his words even and casual, not wanting his friend to worry.

"Don't give me that same, sorry pile of crap, Gray."

Gray smiled at her tone. Despite her tiny size, she could put a five-star general to shame when she barked out orders. "It's nothing to worry about, *Ma'am*. It just seems that there is more than one murderous fiend hiding out in the Underworld. Who would have guessed?"

"Grayson Muir!" Sarah's shrill scream echoed through the line, practically piercing his eardrum. "What the hell is going on down there?"

Gray sighed. She was the only person in the world he'd ever let get away with bossing him around, without fighting tooth and nail. He had learned long ago, there was just no point. Stopping her, was like trying to stop a hurricane. When Sarah Painter found something she wanted, she made it hers, no matter how long it took. When an irritated grunt sounded over the line, Gray gave up all pretenses and quickly launched into a brief rundown of everything that had happened during his brief jaunt into the Underworld. Sarah was suspiciously silent as he recounted their run-in with Povell and his subsequent apprehension. He tried to gloss over his near incineration, but no one had ever accused Sarah of being stupid or slow.

"You are telling me that in the time you've been in the Underworld you have not only caught a murderer but also let said murderer get away with an attempt on your life?"

Gray cringed. "Yes—"

"You dumbass! I let you out of my sight for a couple of hours and you let someone try to murder you? Well, enjoy your freedom while in lasts, *oh mighty omnipotent one*, because when you get back here, I'm never letting you out of my sight again. The team is going to be a full time presence with you from now on, so you better learn to live with it. I'm not willing to keep letting you take these chances with your life. Maybe it doesn't mean that much to you, but it means everything to me. You're my family, you stupid son of a bitch." Sarah's breath hitched, a telltale sign that she was trying to fight back tears.

Remorse swamped Gray. He'd had no idea that his friend had been so worried about his safety. With the situation brought to light, however, he could grudgingly accept that her fear might be justified. "Sarah," he soothed, his voice soft and gentle. "Sweetheart, I'm sorry I've made you worry so much. I've been an idiot. Please, forgive me."

He heard her sniffle. "There's nothing to forgive." She sighed. "You just have to be more careful. It's not just today and all this Demon drama. Things have changed since we first started Revelations. It's time we started acting like it. People know you now. They recognize you and your talent. It's a double-edged sword and we all need to start being more vigilant of the danger."

Gray hated to admit it, but she wasn't wrong. Over the years, as his name and talent had become more widely known, demand for his services had skyrocketed. Unfortunately, the boom in business had brought with it a growing number of people who were not happy about his level of talent. Thieves, murderers, corrupt politicians. Even other Oracles competing for the same piece of the pie. Attempts on his life and threats of violence had been on a gradual rise for years. Gray had turned a blind eye, choosing to ignore it, and assumed everyone else would do the same. Clearly, that assumption had been wrong.

"Agreed. I promise, I will do my very best to make sure that no more evil Demons try to kill me while I'm here. Now, if that's settled," Gray drawled, "are we ready to get back to business, or do you want to keep talking about our feelings and braid each other's hair?"

Sarah snorted. "Prick."

"I know," Gray preened. "It's why all the boys love me."

"You're an idiot." Sarah laughed. "All right, let's get down to business. Tell me what you need."

Within minutes, she had the team put together and had arranged for transport, using a warlock they kept on retainer. A few last checks, and Sarah confirmed that the team would be meeting them in the main receiving hall within the next sixty minutes. With a last shout out from Sarah for good luck, they said their goodbyes and disconnected the call.

Closing the phone, Gray looked up to find Dreo merely feet away, watching him, his lips turned up in amusement.

"What?"

"You are very friendly with your assistant. You care for her."

"Well—yeah. She's my friend, so…we're friendly." Gray tilted his head, curiously. "Is that a problem?"

"As long as you are just friends, there is no problem."

Gray rolled his eyes. "In case you failed to notice, Sarah doesn't have the necessary equipment to get me all hot and bothered. She has those scary girl parts that kind of freak me out." Gray shivered dramatically.

Gray watched a small twitch at the corner of Dreo's mouth as the other man prowled over to him, backing him into a darkened corner. "How fortunate for me. Her loss is my gain." The predatory look in Dreo's eyes combined with the massive bulge in the Demon's pants, had Gray on the edge and trying not to hyperventilate.

"My t-team," Gray stammered. "My team will arrive in the next hour. Once they get here, we will be ready to proceed."

"Excellent." Dreo nodded his approval. "A whole hour, you say? Hmm. With that being the case, what could we possibly do to pass the time?" The Demon pressed his hard body against Gray, trailing a hand down his muscled chest, over his rippled abs, until he reached the growing bulge below his belt.

The noise of the room faded away as Gray felt himself fall under Dreo's spell. He was practically panting as his brain fogged with lust. He knew that this wasn't normal, that there were important things he should be focusing on, but it was difficult when the man before him seemed to have a secret map to all the spots that were guaranteed to get Gray hot, wet and ready to ride. It would be different if the attraction was all one sided, but as their bodies shifted against each other, Dreo's answering hardness pressed, hot and heavy, against Gray's thigh. The knowledge that he was able to illicit such a response from a creature who had experienced more lust and sexual pleasure than Gray could even imagine, had his cock filling with a speed he hadn't thought he was capable of. His cloth-covered dick was hard as steel in seconds. Wiggling slightly, he attempted to maneuver his shaft into a more comfortable position as it tried to fight the confines of its denim prison.

Gray had finally managed to wrangle it down when Dreo shifted, shoving his meaty thigh between Gray's parted legs. The movement pinned Gray's engorged shaft against the unforgiving metal of his zipper, causing him to cry out in pain. The sound of his distress cut through Dreo's ardor. His eyes cleared as his eyebrows pulled together. Reason returned and with it, concern and guilt.

"I'm so sorry," Dreo murmured, his hands rubbing a soothing pattern down Gray's arms. "It seems I let myself get a bit carried away."

"Don't worry about it," Gray dismissed, unsuccessfully trying to hide his wince of discomfort. "*Little Gray* should know better than to get all excited and try to come out to play when we're supposed to be working. I don't know if it's just me, or this place, but for some reason my control is almost nonexistent. Let's just chalk it up to a learning experience, okay?" Gray shook his head, upset and bewildered at his egregious lack of professionalism. Dreo had hired him because of his reputation as Oracle. Gray was embarrassed to say that he was coming off as some kind of flaky, sex-crazed, imposter.

Dreo didn't look convinced. Not wanting to talk about it anymore, Gray pinned Dreo with what Sarah fondly called, the Oracle Death Glare. Dreo looked amused but, when Gray didn't relent, finally threw his hands up in defeat.

"Fine," Dreo groaned. "We'll deal with this later."

"You'd better believe it," Gray muttered, running his hands over his shirt, smoothing out nonexistent wrinkles from the material as he struggled to get his rampant body back under control. It was surprising that, despite the ball numbing pain it had suffered moments earlier, his cock didn't seem willing to give up its demand for release.

It took longer than expected to get his unsatisfied arousal back to a manageable size. After some discreet maneuvering, Gray was no longer in danger of losing his favorite appendage to a lack of blood flow. Looking up, the smirk on Dreo's face had him scowling.

"Everything working out for you, over there?"

"Fuck you, Demon boy."

Dreo chuckled, his eyes warming as he moved closer. "You have that backwards, Oracle...and I most definitely will."

Dragging in a shuttering breath, Gray tried to swallow down the baseball-sized lump in his throat. *Damn. The things this man does to me.* Ignoring the smoldering heat in Dreo's eyes, Gray turned his attention back to the reason for their trip.

"I'd like to do a quick walk through of Lord Lucifer's rooms, if you don't mind." Lifting a brow, he looked at Dreo expectantly.

Dreo watched him for a moment, in silence. He gave a brisk nod and his jaw clenched, but he said didn't say anything else as he turned and made a path through the crowd of gawkers, toward a large oak door near the back of the room. Gray followed him at a fast clip. More guards lined their way as they traveled down a hallway and up two flights of stairs before being led to a room with a massive, ornately carved door that Gray had to assume had belonged to the deceased king. Two more grim-faced guards were stationed outside the room. When they caught sight of Dreo, they instantly straightened to attention.

"At ease, gentleman," Dreo ordered dismissively. "This is the Oracle, Grayson Muir. I have brought him to help us discover the identity of the one responsible for the death of our Lord. He would like to take a look around the room while we wait for his 'team' to arrive."

Gray bite back a smile at the near belligerent way Dreo referred to his guards. He couldn't wait to see his face when they arrived.

Both guards instantly relaxed, the one on the right even going so far as to grace them with a smile. "By all means, enter. If you are here to uncover that murderous snake, we will do anything we can to help you. Lord Lucifer was a good man and a fair ruler. He will be greatly missed by our people. The one responsible for his death will find no friends here."

"Thank you," Gray said. "I promise, I will do everything I can to bring the criminal to justice." With a slight bow to the guards, Gray opened the door and made his way into the chamber of a king.

Entering the room, Gray was blind to his surroundings. While he was sure the expensive furnishings and rich fabrics that filled the space were magnificent, they held no interest for him in that moment. The room itself was what called to him. As soon as he crossed the threshold, his vision dimmed around the edges, the first sign that his *Sight* was manifesting. Without any direction from Dreo, he approached the right side of the bed, intuition telling him that it had been the side the king slept on. Reaching out, he let his hand hover over the surface of the mattress, careful not to make physical contact. He wasn't ready to jump into this vision yet. For now, he was only interested in getting an unbiased impression of his surroundings. Later, he would allow his *Sight* to take over and direct him. His ability to *See* was just one facet of his gift, and not always the most important one.

For the most part, the general public assumed that Oracles were omnipotent. Indestructible, all-knowing gods, able to see anything and everything at the drop of a hat. That couldn't be further from the truth. While Gray would admit he had more control over his abilities than most Oracles, as a whole, Oracles played bitch to their powers more often than not. Visions could strike without notice and once one started, there was no stopping it. Clarity was also an issue. While the message of some visions was as clear as a pane of glass, others were a jumbled mess of colors, images and sound. In those situations, Oracles were forced to use their heightened abilities of deduction and intuition to determine the correct meaning. A correct interpretation, in some situations, could truly mean the difference between life and death. It was for that reason Gray preferred to have as much information as possible before he let himself fall into a vision. Topping it all off was the fact that there were big blank spots in their vision where events might directly influence the Oracle. Omnipotent? Ha! An Oracle's *Sight* was far from an exact science.

A tingle at the back of his neck had Gray fighting back a shiver. An oppressive darkness filled the room. It was a feeling he'd experienced before and was always found in places where murder and betrayal had taken place. There was no doubt in his mind that the king had been murdered. He just had to find out who had committed the crime.

"Is there anything else you wanted to tell me, before I begin?" While additional information wouldn't do anything to change what Gray saw, he always felt it was polite to make the offer. It tended to make those hiring him feel helpful which, in turn, was good for business.

Smirking, Dreo shook his head. "Nothing pertinent to your job. You will, of course, be bringing me along on your vision — as a witness."

It wasn't a question, which immediately got Gray's hackles up. "You don't trust me?"

"Quite the contrary. There are others, however, who will not be so quick to believe the word of an outsider. Demons have long lives and even longer memories. Past grievances are never truly forgotten. For that fact alone, we don't easily trust those outside our race."

"But you trust me?" Disbelief colored Gray's words.

"More than anyone else in the world," Dreo responded.

Gray listened for a sign of mockery or humor in his words, but found none. That realization filled him with a warmth he had never experienced before. Heat pooled in his stomach before heading south to settle in his groin. Perking up at the sensation, his dick filled, ready to see some action. For a moment, he was tempted to give into the feeling.

As an Oracle, he was constantly inundated with all the emotions the world had to offer, both the good and the bad. After a while, he had become numb to them all. It was something all Oracles did because it was one of the few ways to cope with their gift without losing their minds under the constant onslaught. That, combined with the fact that most people immediately doubted the truth of his visions, had made him a bit jaded. Dreo's unquestioning belief was something he'd never experienced before. He just wanted to shut himself away from the world and bask in the novelty of it. Unfortunately, he knew that was not a possibility. Shoring up his resolve, he turned his focus back to the situation at hand.

While he had no problem allowing Dreo to accompany him on his vision, it would have been polite to at least be asked first. His ire grew at the man's highhanded order. Biting back a comment that was sure to get him into trouble, he settled for a stiff nod of agreement. The subtle quirk of Dreo's brow told Gray he hadn't masked his annoyance as well as he'd believed. Oh, well. He couldn't be held accountable for having bitchy thoughts.

Turning away, Gray wandered casually around the room, taking in the rich splendor of his surroundings. Lord Lucifer had obviously been a fan of the arts, as evidenced by the numerous paintings and sculptures placed strategically around the room. When he felt Dreo's dark presence at his back, he struggled to keep his focus on the beauty that surrounded him, but to no avail. The Demon enticed him to the point of distraction. Gray wanted to blame it on Dreo's Lust Demon tendencies, but he knew it would be a lie.

"My team will be here in less than an hour," Gray murmured, his voice surprisingly hoarse. He tried to keep his thoughts on business and not on the overwhelming desire to know what Dreo's body looked like under all those clothes. The clear definition of hard-packed abs though the thin material of Dreo's shirt as it pulled tight across his broad chest was driving Gray to distraction. Licking his lips, he couldn't help but wonder what all the golden skin would taste like. "We should get out of here." He groaned in frustration. "The longer we stay, the more likely it is that I will have a vision. With everything that's happened, I'm not willing to risk that happening without them here to watch my back. If we head back the way we came, we can go wait for them back in the main hall."

Dreo took a step into him, his front pressed flush against Gray's backside, causing Gray's cock to perk up and take notice. Gray could feel Dreo's answering hardness as it pressed, hot and heavy, against his crease. If the size of the bulge prodding his ass was any indication, the Demon was hung like a horse. Gray had never thought of himself as a size queen, but just the thought of Dreo shoving his massive shaft between his swollen lips or drilling it into his tight ass, had him practically coming in his pants.

Giving in to the need building inside him, Gray reached back and ran his palm down Dreo's thick, cloth covered length, before giving it a firm squeeze. The moan that escaped his Demon was music to Gray's ears. He loved a vocal lover, loved that he was able to give such a strong, dominant man enough pleasure to loosen his tightly maintained control. Grabbing a fistful of his dark locks, Dreo jerked Gray's head to the side before leaning down to take his mouth in a brutal kiss. Their meeting was a violent mix of lips, teeth and tongues that left Gray with the faint taste of blood in his mouth. Pulling back when the need for air became too great, Gray gasped for breath, watching Dreo, apprehensively.

"We can't do this..." Gray's words were cut off by a gasp as Dreo buried his face in Gray's neck, sinking his teeth into the muscled flesh of his shoulder. His knees went weak and he nearing lost his footing. Dreo's actions left him feeling off balance and out of control, driving all rational thought from his mind.

"No, Oracle," Dreo hummed. "That's where you're wrong. I'll show you that we can, and will do this. Don't worry about a thing." He thrust forward, allowing his cock to ride the seam of Gray's ass.

"Not...what I...meant," Gray groaned, as Dreo reached around his body and gave his erection a rough rub down. Gray used the last of his willpower to shove Dreo away before things went too far. "What I meant was, we can't do this...*here*. Heightened emotions can affect the residual energy in the room and mess with my powers. If we don't get out of here, we are going to destroy any chance we have of finding out who poisoned your king."

"So, you're not going to try to fight me on this and come up with a hundred reasons why it isn't a good idea and that this isn't a good time?"

"Hell, no!" Gray practically growled. "If you don't fuck me soon, I'm going to explode, and not in a good way. Besides, there's no way I'll be able to have an accurate vision with this kind of lust riding me. At least not without running the risk of destroying all the latent energies in the room. Think of it as a community service," Gray replied eagerly. As soon as he realized what he'd said, he wanted to take the words back. God, could he be any more desperate?

Dreo's lips slowly curled into a wicked smile. "Community service," he smirked. "Is that what the kids are calling it these days?"

Gray's face went beet red. "You know that's not what I mean," he stammered.

"But you said I had to fuck you...that it would be a service to the community?"

"That's not what I meant and you know it," Gray snapped sharply. "You're just being melodramatic ass." He was still irritated with himself. The last thing he needed was to come off needy and pathetic.

Dreo stopped his words with a hard press of lips. Pulling back, he latched a hold of Gray's arm and dragged him toward the door. "Don't worry about a thing, baby. You just come with me. We'll go to my place and take care of you. After all," he leered, "the fate of the world could depend on my ability to fuck you into submission."

Gray didn't even have time to respond, before he found himself being pulled through a maze of winding hallways. Hopefully, he didn't get separated from Dreo. It was bad enough he had taken a pit stop in hell. The last thing he wanted was to make this little side trip a permanent change in zip code.

Chapter Six

After being dragged down more hallways than he could keep track of, Gray finally got a chance to catch his breath when Dreo stopped in front of a plain black door with an elaborate silver knob. It was surrounded by filigreed metal that spanned nearly the whole right edge of the wood, both above and below the handle. Reaching into his pocket, Dreo produced a matching silver key with the same filigree on the handle. Before Gray had a chance to ask any questions, Dreo had the entrance open and practically threw Gray inside. The door slammed shut behind them and they were momentarily plunged into darkness.

Panic started to rise up in Gray, but was squashed a moment later when he heard Dreo make a move to the right, and a soft yellow glow filled the room. At a different time, Gray would have been curious about Dreo's home. Thankfully, with his lust riding him hard, this was not that time.

With nimble fingers, he made quick work of the closure of Dreo's pants and had them pulled down past the man's knees in seconds. As the metal teeth released, Gray was treated to his first look at Dreo's amazing dick. The discovery that Dreo went commando had Gray immediately sinking to his knees, bringing him to eye level with Dreo's more than substantial cock. It had to be the most amazing piece of meat he had ever seen in his life. It was long, thick and uncut, just the way Gray like it. The mushroomed cap was swollen and flushed, nearly purple in color. The slit was weeping copious amounts of pearly fluid, making his mouth water at the thought of getting a taste of the other man's essence.

Bracing himself on Dreo's meaty thighs, Gray looked up into dark eyes burning with an inner glow of hellfire. He was desperate to get the other man's hot dick in his mouth, but he had to be sure this was what Dreo wanted. He had never been one to go where he wasn't wanted.

"Dreo?" He hated the note of pleading in his voice. He had made it a personal pledge to himself to never again beg anyone for anything. The fact that he was so desperate for Dreo that he would throw aside that promise would have worried him, if his need for the man before him wasn't so great.

Dreo's jaw clenched and the tendons of his neck pulled tight, straining against his skin. His hands were fisted at his sides, displaying thick, ropy veins running the length of his forearm. Gray wanted to trace those veins with his tongue. Dreo's nostrils flared and his eyes widened, pupils completely swallowed by the hellfire within. A quick nod of his head gave Gray the permission he required and had him springing into action.

He practically dove at Dreo's crotch, gripping the man's cock in a tight fist before taking it into his waiting mouth. The moment the hot piece of flesh touched his tongue, he was overwhelmed by the dark, musky flavor of the man. Gray had never tasted anything more delicious. Desperate for another taste, he flattened his tongue and laved the fat head of Dreo's dick, urgently suckling the tip, drawing out more of the flavor he craved.

Gray was totally enthralled with his task. When Dreo's heavy hand came down on the back of his head, gripping his hair in a tight fist, he jerked in surprise. Looking up, his mouth still full of cock, Gray was instantly mesmerized by the look of lust on Dreo's face. With his eyelids at half mast, his head thrown back and his long curtain of hair hanging loose around his shoulders, the man was a work of art.

Gray was so lost in the beauty of the sight before him, he didn't realize he had stopped sucking Dreo's cock until a sharp tug of his hair startled him out of his momentary daze. His eyes widened as Dreo's jaw clenched and he used his steely grip to force his shaft farther into Gray's waiting mouth. Excited by the new display of dominance, Gray eagerly swallowed every inch Dreo forced between his stretched lips. Snapping his hips, Dreo started a slow rhythm, in and out of his mouth, gently fucking Gray's swollen lips.

Quickly growing accustomed to the pace, he increased his suction as he tightened his grip on Dreo's muscled thighs. Gray swept his tongue around the flushed head before moving on to tease the weeping slit. He alternated between fluttering licks and gentle nips, knowing it would drive Dreo crazy. After a few minutes, he pulled back, returning his attention to the head, desperate to draw out the dark flavor of his lover. Intoxicated by the musky flavor of the man before him, Gray lost himself in the pleasure of his task. His only thought was to give Dreo so much pleasure, he would loosen the reins on his tightly held control.

A deep, guttural moan escaped the Demon before Gray was forcefully ripped away from his treat and shoved face first against the wall. His fast reflexes saved him from a major case of road rash. A heavy weight pressed against his back and hot breath tickled his ear.

"You should know better than to play these kinds of games, Oracle. This is dangerous." A sharp nip at his lobe was quickly soothed by wet heat, as it was enveloped by Dreo's hot mouth.

"You know us Oracles," Gray gasped, struggling for breath. "We like to live on the edge."

"Is that so?"

"Oh, yeah." He groaned as Dreo gave his shaft a rough pull. "I'm a real wild child."

Dreo grinned. "Well, despite all that, our first time together will not have me shooting my load in your mouth. When I come, it won't be until I'm so deep in your ass, you'll swear you're feeling me tickling the back of your throat. I'm going to mark you so completely that no one will doubt that you belong to me. Everything you are—body, heart, and soul—is mine."

Gray knew he should be afraid. Anyone with half a brain in their head knew how stupid it was to get involved with a Demon. He decided he must have even less brain than that because he couldn't seem to help himself. When it came to this Demon, he had no sense of self-preservation or control.

"And here I thought I was just a passing fancy. I didn't realize you were so interested in me, Lord Demos," Gray countered.

Dreo grinned wickedly. "More than interested, Oracle. I could just eat you up." Dreo licked a line up the side of Gray's neck, emphasizing his point.

Canting his hips, Gray pushed his ass back, allowing the Demon's massive erection to ride his crack. He allowed the man a few thrusts before leaning away, shaking his ass enticingly.

"Well, what are you waiting for? Dinner is served."

There was a second's hesitation before Dreo was on him, tearing at his clothes in a flurry groping hands and ripping fabric. Before he had time to register what was happening, Dreo had his clothing in a pile at his feet and was watching him, naked hunger burning in his eyes. Without a thought, Gray arched his back, presenting his ass to Dreo's hungry gaze. With no further encouragement needed, Dreo dropped to his knees, his hand immediately going to Gray's ass. Gripping his cheeks with both hands, Dreo spread him open, exposing his most private place for his perusal. Cool air hit his puckered flesh, causing it to clench in reflex.

"Beautiful," Dreo breathed against his skin. A stream of hot air skating across the heated skin of his crack had his pink star twitching and rippling in need. When Gray felt the hot, wet pressure of Dreo's tongue at his entrance, he almost came out of his skin. There was no hesitation in the man's movements, but honestly, what would you expect from a lust Demon? Dreo gently fluttered his tongue around the outside edge of his entrance, moisture from his exploration pooling at Gray's opening, expertly relaxing the guardian muscle. Soft licks turned into probing thrusts as Dreo pointed his tongue, spearing it into Gray's ass, delving in as deep as he could go.

Gray groaned, low and deep, as Dreo's carnal assault left him defenseless in the wake of such pleasure. He had never experienced anything like it. Gray was far from a virgin, but he had never had a lover take control of his body and dominate him so completely before. It was as if Dreo had an inside line to his libido and knew exactly what Gray wanted without him ever having to ask. On second thought, as a lust Demon, maybe he did. Gray couldn't find the energy to care, either way. He was too lost in the pleasure of Dreo's tongue owning his ass to question the origin of Dreo's skills. As Dreo forced his invading muscle to new depths within him, Gray writhed on the end of his tongue, a slave to the sensations the Demon had awakened within him.

Dreo brought Gray to the edge, over and over, never granting him the mercy of release. Gray was convinced the Demon was trying to make him lose his mind, as his need grew to a level he had never experienced before. He tried, and failed, to bite back a whimper as he was denied release, yet again. A low chuckle sounded from behind him.

"Finally."

Without warning, Dreo withdrew his tongue, leaving his hole momentarily grasping and empty. Quickly, he blanketed himself against Gray's back, placed the fat head of his cock against Gray's entrance and thrust forward. The force of the movement drove the air from Gray's lungs, leaving him breathless. Heat seared through his ass as pain and pleasure melded together, leaving him unable to think. Dreo's cock was even bigger than he had expected, leaving him with the feeling that he had been impaled by someone's fist. Groaning and whimpering, he tried to pull away from the invading flesh. Dreo's arm came around his chest as his other hand gripped his hip, effectively locking him in place.

"Easy, now," Dreo soothed. "Just give yourself a minute to get used to me."

"No..." Gray moaned pitifully. "Too big...can't fit..."

"Yes, it will," Dreo answered, sharply. "You've got more than half of me already. Just a bit more to go. You were made for me. You were made to take my cock. Now, take a breath and relax for me."

Gritting his teeth, Gray tried to do what Dreo asked. Taking a deep breath, he forced air into his depleted lungs and tried to coax his stiff muscles into accepting the invading girth. Unfortunately, the minute Dreo tried to thrust deeper, Gray's muscles clenched tight, once again fighting to keep him out.

Dreo growled behind him, sending a new wave of lust through his body. "I told you to relax!"

"I'm trying." Gray gritted his teeth as Dreo tried to forge ahead, again, meeting with the same results.

"You will obey your mate," Dreo ordered, delivering a sharp slap to Gray's right cheek, shocking him to his core. In all his years, he had never been spanked by a lover. He was so stunned, he didn't realize he'd relaxed slightly until he felt Dreo's dick inch deeper inside him. Focusing on the sensations elicited by his new depth, Gray was unprepared for the slap that landed on his other cheek. A groan escaped him as heat burned through his bottom.

"Your ass looks amazing, blushing such a beautiful red from my hand. You love it, don't you? Tell me that you love the feeling of me spanking you."

Gray's first instinct was to deny Dreo's words, but he couldn't force the words from his mouth. As the warmth from his bottom spread through the rest of his body, he had to admit he didn't hate the feeling. After the initial shock from the blow wore off, it actually started to feel pretty damn good.

Dreo seemed to take his lack of answer as a challenge. Gray had no time to prepare as his lover began to rain blows down on his ass, his cock still firmly embedded in Gray's backside. There was no pattern to Dreo's strikes, as he alternated their force and location, effectively keeping Gray in a constant state of awareness. Before Gray knew it, he was pushing back to meet the blows, moaning as the heat burned through him.

He was so overcome with the new sensations rolling through him, he didn't register the fact that his body had relaxed further until he felt Dreo's balls slap against his ass. He was amazed by his body's reaction to the other man's dominance. He took a breath, trying to relax around the new feeling of Dreo inside him. He'd never had a lover so deep or who filled him so entirely. The feeling was both amazing and terrifying.

Mercifully, Dreo seemed to sense his state of mind and waited for him to make the first move. After a few deep breathes, Gray pushed back into his impalement, slowly fucking himself onto Dreo's cock. They moaned, in unison, as the most intense pleasure Gray had ever experienced washed over him.

"So good," he breathed, shoving back against Dreo's cock. "More!"

Dreo huffed out a laugh. "You don't give the orders here, Oracle."

"Please," Gray moaned desperately.

"Damn! You beg so beautifully. If we had more time, I'd leave you like this for hours. Teetering on the brink of climax, never quite able to slip over the edge. You are so gorgeous like this."

"Dreo..."

"Hush." Dreo silenced him with a devouring kiss, pushing his tongue between Gray's gasping lips. He licked and tasted every inch of Gray's mouth before the need for air forced him to withdraw.

Dreo chose that moment to take back control of their lovemaking. He increased the speed of his thrusts, leaving Gray still struggling to draw air back into his lungs. Snapping his hips, he slammed into Gray over and over again. The sound of slapping skin and Gray's cries filled the air, echoing against the stone walls. Gray was beyond the point of conscious thought. All he could do was brace himself for whatever Dreo doled out.

"So fucking tight," Dreo growled against his ear. "So perfect. So mine." Dreo pounded into him harder and Gray could only groan in response.

Reaching around his waist, Dreo jacked Gray's dick at a fevered pace. "Are you ready for what I have for you? When I tell you, you're going to come all over my hand."

Unable to form words, Gray managed to nod his head, fervently, prepared to beg for what Dreo held just out of his reach. If he didn't get to come soon, he feared he was in very real danger of becoming a victim of spontaneous combustion. Panting, he tried to force himself back, desperate to get as much of Dreo's monster cock inside him as possible. If he could take him all maybe, just maybe, his hot shaft would rub where he needed it so bad.

A sharp slap to his ass jolted him out of his fantasy and back to the present. He looked over his shoulder and into eyes, set aglow with hellfire. The room around them was awash in light from the fiery, glowing orbs. The expression on Dreo's face was cool and calculating. Gray's inability to read the man who was mastering him so completely set his nerves on edge was well as kicked his arousal into overdrive.

"I think you still have a lesson to learn about who is in charge here," Dreo stated sternly. "I look forward to teaching it to you, when we have more time." Gripping Gray's hip with a bruising force, Dreo placed a quick kiss on the back of his neck before plowing back into his abused hole.

Dreo rode his ass like he owned it, and if Gray was being honest with himself, he had never enjoyed anything more. No one had ever dared to take control and possess him so entirely, before. Gray never would have allowed it. With every thrust, he could feel the thick veins on Dreo's shaft dragging along his channel, sending fissures of electricity up his spine. He could feel his release building again and knew there would be no stopping it this time around.

"Dreo... Gonna come..." Gray warned, gasping for breath.

"Damn right you are!" Tightening his grip, Dreo pounded into Gray with a force that would have scared him if he'd been in his right mind. With his brain fogged with lust, all he could do was hang on and enjoy the ride. Dreo was jerking his cock so fast, Gray knew he was going to be raw tomorrow, but couldn't find the strength to care.

"Come, Gray. Now!" Dreo's words registered to his ears at the same time he felt the man's shaft swell within in him, signaling his own burgeoning release. Gray had never been able to come on command, but something about this Demon seemed to change all the rules. Without a thought, Gray's balls pulled up tight and he was spraying the stone wall with a thick layer of pearly cream. Seconds later, he felt his ass heat, as his insides were bathed with Dreo's steamy release.

Groaning, Dreo collapsed against his back, his breathing erratic. The heavy weight of the man was surprisingly comforting, as Gray tried to calm his own racing heart. He'd never been much for cuddling, but he was starting to think he could get used to it, if this powerful Demon was the one holding him tight. From the sounds of it, he had a feeling that there were a lot of things he was going to have to get used to in regards to his new lover.

Chapter Seven

"Damn," Dreo panted against his neck. "Are you sure you don't have a Lust Demon somewhere in your family tree? Maybe a Siren or an Incubus? That was amazing!"

Gray tensed. Straightening, he pushed away from Dreo and began looking around the room for his discarded clothing. He knew Dreo didn't hadn't meant anything by it, but just the mention of his 'family' made his blood run cold. Despite his determination to not let their abandonment hurt him, he still had moments where it became a heavy weight on his chest.

The sensation of being watched had Gray looking up to see Dreo staring at him, a curious expression on his face. Sighing, he knew he was going to have to give the man some kind of explanation for his behavior. Grabbing his underwear off the floor, he focused on cleaning himself up, not able to meet Dreo's perceptive gaze.

"I don't know anything about my family. I was left outside a fire station when I was an infant. No family ever came forward to claim me, so I became a ward of the state."

"Grayson," Dreo murmured softly. Grabbing Gray's wrist, he pulled him into a bone crushing embrace. "I'm sorry. I had no idea."

"I know," Gray responded flatly, suddenly feeling very foolish. "There's no way you could have known. It's just a touchy subject for me. I shouldn't have been such a prick about it."

Looking away from Dreo, Gray grabbed his shirt and pants from the floor then hurriedly finished dressing. There was no way he wanted to be naked while they talked about his lack of family. He felt vulnerable, and that was an emotion he avoided at all costs. It was a weakness that left you open to attack. Gray had learned that lesson, well. He had made it his personal mission to never be weak again.

Once dressed, he turned his attention back to Dreo. The Demon's expression was equal parts curiosity and confusion. It was obvious the man had questions, but he was too polite to voice them. Gray groaned. He knew he would have to allow the man to ask his questions. While he didn't understand the connection he felt to the Demon, he knew he could trust him.

Gray sighed. "Just ask."

"So when you say no family, you mean—"

"I mean, *no family*," Gray emphasized. "I was first brought to Burgus House. It is an orphanage that houses small children. I lived there until I was around six years old, then I was transferred to a group home, Milton Hall. I lived there until I aged out at eighteen, and I've been on my own ever since."

Dreo scowled. "I don't understand. I thought human couples were clamoring to adopt babies. How is it that you stayed in the system your entire life without being placed with a family?"

Gray laughed, but there was no joy in it. "From what I've been told, even as a baby, people could tell I was...different. One of the women who worked at the orphanage was convinced I was possessed or something. She was the reason I was transferred to the group home, so young. Group homes are like a dorm, so they don't like to move kids there until they're older, usually teenagers. In my case, I guess they thought it would be okay to make an exception. I mean, when the head of the orphanage caught the woman holding me under water in a bath tub, trying to force the devil out of me, I don't think that she felt she had any other choice but to move me out of the building, for my own safety."

"What happened to the woman?" Dreo asked, quietly.

"I think she still works at the orphanage," Gray replied dismissively. "I'm not really sure." In all honesty, he hadn't given the woman a lot thought after he'd been removed from the orphanage.

"Are you fucking kidding me?" Dreo roared. "She should have had her ass thrown in jail. The woman tried to kill you!"

Gray shrugged. Honestly, what could he say? He knew Dreo had a valid point. Gray had questioned it himself, after being forced to move to the group home. He'd been angry and scared. His immediate relocation had left him feeling like he had done something wrong — that he had deserved what had happened to him. The group home had seemed more like a prison sentence than a safe haven.

It hadn't taken long for him to change his way of thinking. While it wasn't the homelike environment he had been used to, the group home had offered him something he had never experienced before—freedom. With no one watching his every move, he'd been able to make his own decisions for the first time in his life. It'd been then that he'd decided it was time to put all the pain and guilt behind him, and just accept things the way they were. There was no sense concerning himself with things he couldn't change and he had plenty of other things to worry about as it was.

At that time in his life, he'd had to focus all his energy on just trying to stay sane. It was then that his abilities had truly started to manifest. His visions, which had been sporadic at best, had started to increase in strength and frequency. He'd never admitted it to anyone but, when the visions had first occurred, he had begun to believe the woman at the orphanage had been right about him. That belief had filled him with an overwhelming sense of self-loathing. He'd been so convinced of the evil within himself that, at one point, he'd tried to kill himself to rid the world of his evil.

Looking back, that had been the point where his visions had taken on a more violent cast. He'd found out later, through speaking with other Oracles who had had similar experiences, that the gift grew in stages. They had all gone through periods where violent, disturbing images filled their visions, only to then go through periods where everything they saw was good and pure. They referred to it as 'the settling', when their powers grew and settled into them, like putting on layers of clothing, one on top of the other. Eventually, their powers stabilized, blending together seamlessly.

He looked up at Dreo, whose eyes were still filled with a murderous rage at his past treatment. A warm wave of pleasure washed over him with the realization that such a powerful man could have any sort of feelings for him. The Demon's outrage, although unnecessary, tugged at his heart.

"It is what it is, Dreo. It's in the past and no good will come from dredging it all back up now. Besides, I thought you brought me down here for a reason. My team should be here soon, and we need to get ready to meet them."

Dreo looked ready to argue, but at the last minute, seemed to bite his tongue. He settled for throwing a glare at Gray before retrieving his own clothes, dressing in quick, jerky movements. After spending another few minutes putting the room back to rights, they headed back to the main receiving hall to wait for Gray's team.

A crowd had gathered by the time they returned to the hall. Demon men, women and children were gathered at the center of the room, surrounding what Gray assumed was his team. His men never failed to make a lasting impression. Pushing his way through the assembled masses, Gray smiled as he caught sight of the eight weapon-laden men standing in the center of the room, seemingly unfazed by the number of Demons congregating around them. There were many curious faces in the crowd, obviously wondering about what kind of excitement these new visitors might have in store for them. After the show Gray had provided so far, he could hardly blame them.

Breaking into a run, Gray crossed the room, zeroing in on a large man standing slightly in front of the rest. The man was obviously their leader, but that had nothing to do with his size. The aura the man exuded practically screamed alpha. If that wasn't enough to tip someone off about what he was, the golden gleam in his eyes cleared up any confusion.

Gray sensed Dreo's steps falter behind him, but didn't slow his approach. As he reached the group, the leader opened his arms wide, allowing Gray to leap into his embrace. The man's thick arms wrapped around him, cocooning him in a reassuring warmth. Gray sighed, releasing some of the tension that had built in him from his earlier conversation with Dreo.

"Gray." The man's voice boomed, low and rough.

Tilting his head back, Gray beamed up at him. "Maddox, it's good to see you. I'm glad you're here. Where's Stephen? Didn't he come with you?"

"Nah. He's still working that murder case with Detroit PD. He sounded like he was in the middle of something when I called. I gave him an update on the situation and let him know where we'd be. He said to call if we needed him. I told him that it shouldn't be necessary and to focus on his case."

Gray nodded his agreement. "He needs to stay where he can do the most good. We can handle this without him."

Stephen Jurgens was a well-known psychic and a close friend of Gray's. It was widely known that he worked for Revelations on an 'as needed' basis. What wasn't common knowledge was that he was also the man responsible for saving Gray's life when he had been on the verge of ending it. Stephen had talked him down from that ledge, figuratively speaking, and Gray would always be grateful. He'd shown him not only how to control his powers so they no longer ran roughshod over him, but how to hone them so they could be used to help those in need. There was no way Gray would never be able to repay Stephen for what he'd done, but he planned to spend the rest of his life trying.

Lost in his thoughts, Gray almost didn't notice the growl that sounded behind him and echoed through the room. Startled, Gray pulled back, looking over his shoulder for its source. Dreo stood mere inches from him, his eyes glowing blood red as hellfire practically leaped from their depths. Gray felt a hand on his shoulder, before he was roughly jerked away from the Demon.

"Wolf..." Dreo growled, hands fisted at his side. He dropped his shoulders, clearly readying himself for attack.

"Demon," Maddox countered.

"Release my mate, dog, before I forget our people are at peace and skin your mangy hide!"

"Be careful who you call a dog, Demon. I might decide to show you the distinction." Turning away from Dreo, Maddox looked down at Gray, surprise clear in the Shifter's eyes. "Mate?"

Gray felt his cheeks heat under his scrutiny. "It's a long story," he answered irritably. "Can we talk about this later?"

The man smirked. "Sure, Gray, it can wait. I can't wait to hear that story. Who would have thought— little Gray, settling down with one guy. I guess stranger things have happened. Are you positive this is really the guy for you?" Maddox pulled Gray closer in a mock embrace. "Maybe we should test the theory?"

Dreo took a step forward, his whole body vibrating in fury. "Don't even think about it! He is *my* mate. Now, get your hands off of him before I rip off your fucking arm!"

Gray saw Maddox stiffen and knew he had to do something before one of the men he cared about got hurt. Stepping away from his friend, Gray went to Dreo, wrapping his arms around the man in, what he hoped, was a reassuring embrace.

"Dreo, I'd like you to meet Maddox Blackwood, Alpha of the Pontiac Pack and one of my oldest friends. Mad, this is Andreo Demos. He is the Demon who hired me for this job." He would have stopped there, but when Dreo started growling again, he knew that wasn't going to be an option. "We are also seeing each other." Dreo still looked angry, but at least he stopped his rabid dog impression.

Maddox stared at them silently for a moment, before his mouth quirked up into a grin. "A mate, huh? Damn, Gray. You sure move fast. I can't wait to tell Dad. Congrats, man!"

"Thanks," Gray replied grudgingly. "I'm still undecided on the whole mate thing, but I'm willing to take things slow and see how it goes. Until then, I'd rather people not make a big deal about it."

Maddox cocked a brow at him skeptically. "I know you don't get it because you were brought up around humans, so you weren't raised to believe in mating and destined mates, but it isn't something you 'try out' to see if it works. When it comes to mating, you don't get a choice, Gray. You either are, or you're not. If you are, you better come to grips with it, because, barring death, there's no getting out of it."

Smiling smugly, Dreo wrapped a possessive arm around his shoulder, pulled him in and planted a hard kiss on his lips. The moment their lips touched, Gray was powerless to fight against him. He was lust, and heat and unfilled need. The idea of pulling away never even crossed his mind, not even when black spots began to appear before his eyes. Dreo's expression was full of male arrogance. "You are finally beginning to understand. We are mates, Grayson Muir. You are mine — forever."

The cocky grin Dreo flashed in his direction left Gray fighting back the urge to punch the arrogant Demon in the face. Scowling, he watched Dreo swagger away toward a contingent of Demon guards skirting the edge of the crowd.

"Forever could be a lot shorter than he thinks. I think I could take him. He has to sleep sometime." Gray didn't even try to hide his annoyance.

Laughing, Maddox placed a reassuring hand on his shoulder before turning back to the rest of the team. Motioning them forward, he called out a few last minute orders before turning his attention back to Gray, his expression all business.

"We ready to get started?"

Relief washed over him. He could have kissed Maddox for the distraction. The mess of conflicting emotions inside him was not conducive to *Seeing*. He needed to be centered, totally focused on the task at hand. Taking a breath, he closed his eyes, cleared his thoughts and opened himself up to his gift. In layman's terms, he was laying out the welcome mat and leaving the front door unlocked. The sooner he finished the job, the sooner he could go home and gain a little space between him and his Demonic stalker.

Prepared to wait the requisite few minutes for his powers to acknowledge him, Gray was shocked when, almost instantly, he felt his gift respond to his call. It was a reaction that usually took a great deal of focus to achieve. This time, it was like his Oracle abilities were just waiting to be used.

Despite his shock, he was pleased when he opened his eyes and saw fog edging in on the periphery of his vision, as well as the brighter cast of the room and its inhabitants. Both were signs of the manifestation of his gift, but he had never had a reaction this strong before. The room was practically glowing. Possibly a reaction to using his powers in the Underworld? Gray shook his head. It was a worry best saved for another time. Looking up, he found Dreo was back and staring at him — mouth open and eyes wide.

"What?"

"Your eyes..." Dreo murmured. "I've never seen anything like it. They're beautiful."

Gray snorted. Spinning on his heel, he started across the room, heading back toward the murdered Lord's chambers. He knew what Dreo was seeing and, while his eyes had been called many things, not once had they been called beautiful. Odd, freaky, terrifying and grotesque were the most common descriptions, but there were many more out there, each more hurtful than the last. When tapping into his *Sight*, his normally dark green eyes paled to a milky white, with a light ring of green were the iris should be. Add to that, the fact that they glowed faintly when in a vision, and he was a perfect candidate for a side show freak. Just set him up a booth, between the Bearded Lady and the Elephant Man, and he'd be good to go. *Come one, come all! Witness the horror that is…The Oracle!*

A heavy hand fell on Gray's shoulder, jerking him out of his inner whine-fest, and into a hard embrace. Looking up, he instinctively knew it would have been Dreo who'd approached him, despite his obvious bad mood. Gray knew he tended to be a bit emotionally high-maintenance. His issues weren't news to anyone who truly knew him. When he was in one of his moods, people gave him space. They assumed it was best to let him work things out on his own. In reality, it couldn't be further from the truth. Solitude only caused him to withdraw further, putting up walls against everyone, until he was unreachable.

Dreo was different. He saw through the smoke and mirrors, right to the heart of the situation. Even after knowing the man for a matter of a few days, he already understood more about the way Gray worked, than many of his closest friends and associates.

"Kiss me," Dreo demanded, gripping his jaw firmly, denying him any chance of escape.

"No," Gray whined petulantly. "We don't have time for this." He was ashamed of his childish tone, but he needed something between himself and the gorgeous Demon. The man saw too much, able to cut through Gray's normal bullshit and see through to everything he tried to hide. It left Gray feeling entirely too exposed.

Dreo wrapped an arm around his waist, bringing Gray into his hard body. When Gray tried to move away, Dreo held him tighter, allowing him to struggle. He strained against the hold until the fight finally left him. With his strength gone, he collapsed into Dreo's waiting arms.

"It's all right," Dreo crooned, softly. "I've got you."

"But we've got to find out who—"

Dreo covered Gray's lips with his hand, effectively silencing rest of his words. "We have all the time in the world. It's not like the man is going to get any more dead. You are The Oracle. Without you, none of this would be possible. If you need a few minutes to calm down, you have them. Anything you need, all you have to do is ask."

The soft brush of lips against Gray's mouth was unexpected, but it was the look in Dreo's eyes that left him struggling for breath. Gray was no stranger to lust. He had experienced it often and was used to seeing it in the eyes of his lovers. Dreo was different. When Dreo looked at him, Gray saw more than he'd ever thought possible. The lust was there, but burning even more brightly was a love that could not be disguised. It shone out for everyone to see. It filled Gray with both tremendous joy and ball-numbing fear.

Understanding softened Dreo's features as the man took a step back. "This can wait until later. For now, let's focus on the job. Once that's done, we will have plenty of time to explore what is growing between us."

"Jesus," Maddox groaned, pushing his way between them as he began to march down the hall in the wrong direction. "Don't you two ever stop? We've got a job to do, in case you forgot."

"You're just jealous," Gray snarked with a toss of his head.

"You're probably right, but it doesn't change the fact that we were hired to do a job and we need to get it done. Now, if you'll hurry up maybe we can get this done quickly so I don't miss my shows."

Gray rolled his eyes. Heaven forbid Maddox miss a rerun of one of the numerous crime shows he religiously watched. "We'd probably get done a lot quicker if you were heading the right direction, don't you think?" Gray asked smugly.

Jerking to a stop, Maddox glared at Gray over his shoulder. "You know, sometimes I think I could kill you, hide the body and no one would be the wiser." His voice was a grouchy, low rumble.

Gray laughed. "You know that's not true. Your parents would notice that I was missing in less time than it would take them to realize that you were missing. They love me best."

Maddox scowled. "You're probably right."

"There's no probably about it. I'm loveable, they can't help themselves." Gray squinted at his friend. "Maybe if you tried not being such a prick all the time, they would like you more."

"Yeah?" Maddox snarled. "Or maybe I just get rid of your obnoxious ass and they would quit trying to make me be more like you, yeah?"

Laughing, Gray turned away and continued down the hall leaving Maddox and the rest of his team to fan out around him in defensive positions. He doubted the president had better security than he did. Thinking about it, though, it did kind of make sense. You could always elect another president. Oracles, on the other hand, were basically an endangered species. As they neared the dead king's chambers, an unsettling sense of foreboding fell over him. What had previously seemed like a mundane task, now took on an aura of menace.

"Something's different."

Dreo jerked to a stop, his eyes immediately going to Gray's face. "What do you mean?"

"I don't know," Gray murmured hesitantly. "It just feels...different. Like something's changed. I don't know how to explain it any better than that."

Dreo watched him, his jaw clenched and his expression serious. After a moment, he straightened to his full height, determination replacing his previous concern. "It changes nothing. We still have to get to the bottom of this and chose a new Lord of the Underworld. Everyone will just have to be more vigilant. Hopefully, if we remain on guard, we will be able to head off any danger."

With that said, Dreo continued toward the royal chamber, his shoulders back, his stance as regal as any king. Surrounded by his guards, he was a fearsome sight to behold. Gray hoped that they were strong enough to face whatever evil was dogging their steps. Following after Dreo, the sensation of unease grew stronger. As they approached the door, Gray hoped he was just experiencing a bad case of nerves and not a prediction of things to come.

Chapter Eight

When they reached the king's chamber, the team spread out, scanning the area for danger. Maddox and Dreo went over and spoke with the same two guards, who were stationed at the door. A few hushed words were spoken before the men came back.

"Colton said that no one has been by here since we left, let alone gone into the room." Dreo's tone was cool, yet soothing.

"I don't care what he says," Gray answered dismissively. "There is something different. Whether it was caused by a person, a thing or a phase of the moon, I don't know. All I do know is that something is different from when we were here last time. Darker. More threatening."

Dreo watched Gray before sparing a glance over at Maddox, who merely shrugged. Gray fought a smile. His friend knew better than to dismiss one of Gray's feelings. Those feelings had kept them out of more trouble than either of them probably cared to remember.

After another glance around, Dreo turned to him. "I know you don't have a good feeling about this and I don't want you to think that I don't believe you, but it doesn't change the fact that we have to go inside that room to find out what happened to Lucifer. You have to trust that I won't let anything happen to you, okay?" Dreo looked at him, his expression beseeching. "I promise. I will keep you safe."

Leaning down, Dreo placed a brief kiss on Gray's forehead before turning his attention back to his men. The guards gave the hall one last look before Maddox and his second in command, Ben, moved in and entered the chamber. A few minutes later, they called out, signaling that it was safe for the rest to enter.

Walking into the room, Gray could immediately feel the change in the air. Reaching out with his gift confirmed what he'd already sensed. "Someone was here."

Dreo's head jerked up, confusion clear on his face. "What do you mean, someone was here? We haven't even been out of the room a half hour and there are guards posted all along the corridor leading to Lord Lucifer's chambers."

"Someone had to have come in after we left to meet the team. I can sense them. They did something to muddle the residual energies here. There isn't enough of the original energy left to get a clear read on whoever murdered your king."

"You've got to be kidding me!" Dreo snarled, face molten with rage. "How is that even possible?"

Gray shrugged. It was a question he would also like an answer to. As events unfolded, he was becoming more and more concerned. The fact that the intruder knew exactly what to do to hinder Gray's power was worrisome. Because of their rareness, Oracles tended to be enigmatic. It would take someone with an intimate knowledge of Oracles and their powers to disrupt the energies to the point that not even Gray could get a reading from them. The list of people who would have access to that kind of information was incredibly small.

As Gray began working through all the possibilities, an idea started to grow in his mind. He didn't want to acknowledge it. Gray would have preferred to discount it as an impossibility. Unfortunately, the more he thought about it, the more sense it made. To have so much knowledge of Oracles, there was truly only one possibility.

"An Oracle," Gray muttered to himself.

"Excuse me?"

"It has to be an Oracle. Probably working with someone else—my guess would be a Demon. It's the only thing that makes sense and it explains the complete destruction of all of the residual energy in the room. It's the only way to hide something so completely that not even an Oracle can *See* it. If you haven't noticed, Oracles don't like to advertise any weaknesses. No one, other than another Oracle, would know how to do it."

"I don't understand. Why would it have to be an Oracle?"

Gray sighed, searching for an explanation that Dreo would understand. "Being an Oracle is kind of like that movie *Fight Club*. The first rule of being an Oracle is that no one talks about being an Oracle. There are too few of us. It was decided, long ago, to keep the knowledge a closely guarded secret." Running fingers through his hair, Gray struggled with how much to tell Dreo. "There are no books you can read, or classes to take. The only way to learn about Oracles is from an

Oracle. My own training was mostly trial and error. If it hadn't been for my friend, Stephen, finding me, I wouldn't have even known what I was."

"Is Stephen an Oracle?" Dreo inquired.

"No. Stephen Jurgens is a psychic. Thankfully, he had worked with a few Oracles in the past, so when he found me, he recognized what I was and contacted them for help. While they wouldn't tell him much, they told him enough to keep me from going out of my mind. Beyond that, I was on my own."

"Would this Stephen know how to alter the energy in the room?" Dreo asked suspiciously.

Gray shook his head vehemently. "No, and even if he did, he doesn't have the ability to totally erase the energy from the room. At best, he might be able to distort a vision, but the information would still be there, just harder to see." Gray met Dreo's gaze, his eyes pleading for his Demon to believe him. "I know what I'm talking about, Dreo. Please, trust me."

"Of course, I believe you," Dreo growled, not an ounce of hesitation in his voice. "We just need to be sure before we make a move on this. There are a lot of powerful Demons down here, and right now most of them are vying to be the new Lord of the Underworld. We will need to be cautious until we are ready to move against the murderer."

Turning his attention to the others in the room, Dreo began barking out orders. Authority practically oozed from the man's pores. He was born to be a leader. Gray was curious to know if Dreo was one of the Demons hoping to become the new ruler of the Underworld. He definitely had the personality for it.

Gray noticed Dreo watching him from across the room. His cheeks immediately flamed, embarrassment burning through him at being caught staring like a starry-eyed school girl. A smirk graced the man's lips as he made his way across the room.

Dreo stopped with mere inches separating them. Close enough that Gray could feel the warmth emanating from his hard body. The man put off heat like a furnace, probably from the hellfire that was forever smoldering within him. Reaching down, Dreo cupped Gray's face with his large, calloused hands. The move was surprisingly gentle for such a big man.

"You've been thinking pretty hard over here," Dreo muttered softly as his thumb traced lightly across Gray's full bottom lip. "What is going on in that busy brain of yours?"

Without giving Gray a chance to respond, Dreo took his mouth in a devouring kiss. Forcing his tongue between Gray's parted lips, he explored the cavern of his mouth, leaving no inch untasted. Gray was no idle bystander, giving as good as he got. Their tongues dueled in a flurry of lips, teeth and tongues. Strong hands held his hips in a bruising grip, causing his hard cock to grind against Dreo's muscled thigh. There was so much yearning in Dreo's kiss, Gray knew he would never get enough of this man. The passion of Dreo's kiss caused heat to build within him, until he was a writhing, moaning mess in the Demon's arms. Dreo groaned, low and rough, before pushing Gray up against the cool, stone wall. They were both so lost in the passion building between them, they lost track of everything else around them, until a throat being cleared nearby froze them in their tracks.

Pulling away from Dreo's mouth, Gray looked over his shoulder and into the room, still filled with his own team, as well as Dreo's Demon guards. Maddox, smiling like a lunatic, gave him a little finger wave. Shame and humiliation burned away any residual lust as Gray fought futilely to keep the blush from his cheeks.

Maddox laughed. "Not that we weren't enjoying the show, guys—'cause let's face it, that was smokin' hot—but what's the plan?"

"Gray?" Dreo looked at him expectantly.

"I think we need to focus on the Oracle. Oracles are few and far between. We're right up there with albino kangaroos on the rarity scale. Add to that the fact that whoever it is was willing to team up with a Demon, and we should be able to cut the list down to a handful of possibilities."

"What do you mean, 'willing to team up with a Demon'? Do you have a problem with Demons?" Balen, the Demon Dreo had spoken with when they'd arrived, stepped forward, glowering down at Gray.

"Me, personally? Not as much anymore, but I'm need to work on it. The world, as a whole? Yes."

Balen's lips thinned and his face turned nearly purple with rage. Yeah, the man was pissed. Thankfully, the anger pumping through him had rendered him temporarily speechless. Gray didn't wait for him to recover, not wanting to extend the confrontation any longer than necessary.

"Look. Justified or not, Demons don't have the best reputation around. People believe that you're dangerous—a fact that I don't believe is completely false, no matter how much you'd like to claim otherwise. Nevertheless, most people, para or human, aren't willing to take that chance, so they won't work with you."

"I don't see what that has to do with Oracles," Balen interrupted.

Gray sighed. "Because of our small numbers, Oracles are even more cautious than most. Our job set isn't designed to make everyone happy. We see the truth of things. When the truth rivals what people want to believe, they have a tendency to get a bit...disgruntled. Not many Oracles would be willing to ignore the rumors about your people. Besides myself, I have heard of three or four others, worldwide, willing to take that kind of risk."

"And yet you are willing to take that risk?" Balen sneered.

Gray shrugged. "What can I say? I guess I'm just the bad boy of the Oracle world."

Maddox coughed out a laugh, and Gray had to bite his cheek to keep the smile off his face at Balen's expression of pure annoyance. When he'd accepted this job, he hadn't realized that Demons were so stuffy and fun to mess with. If he had, he might have agreed to go to Hell all those times Sarah had wished him there.

Dreo stepped between them, his lips pulled down in irritation. "If you two are done, we do still have murderer to find. I would appreciate it if you could both manage to act like adults for the duration." He didn't allow any room for disagreement as he turned away to confer with the assembled guards.

"Your smart mouth finally got you into a bit of trouble, didn't it?"

Maddox's smile was huge. Gray knew his friend was right, but that didn't mean that he had to like it. Unfortunately, the Alpha in his friend didn't allow for Maddox to be a humble victor.

"Would it kill you to be a little less of a prick?" Gray scowled.

"Probably not, but then how would I have any fun?"

"I thought maturity was supposed to come with age? I'm pretty sure I haven't seen any sign of it in you. Does it skip a generation?"

"Nope. I'm pretty sure I got vaccinated against it, when I was younger."

"When you were just a puppy? Do they administer that before or after the heartworm pills?"

"After, of course. Everybody knows that."

Gray and Maddox stared at each other in silence. Gray was surprised by the lack of chatter in the room until he noticed that everyone was staring at them, mouths hanging open in disbelief. Looking back to his friend, he saw that Maddox had also noticed their audience. Quirking a lopsided grin, Mad shrugged sheepishly.

"Who would have guessed that we would be the most interesting thing in the room?"

Unable to hold it back, Gray's laughter echoed through the room. The deep, joyful sound seemed to lighten the oppressive feeling that hung in the air, allowing everyone to breathe a bit easier. While some of the Demon guards still stared at them in shock, the members of his own team were used to such displays. They merely shook their heads and chuckled right along with him.

A throat cleared and Gray looked up into the dark, heated eyes of Andreo Demos. A warm hand grabbed him, wrapped gently around his throat in a primal display of ownership. There was no pressure or pain, just the reassurance that Dreo was there and everything would be all right. Gray shivered, unable to hide his reaction to the Demon's touch. He swallowed hard, then moaned as Dreo squeezed slightly, not to cause harm but to reassert his dominance.

"Are you ready, Oracle?"

"Ready for what?" Gray frowned.

"To lead our men." Dreo cocked his head and confusion shone in his eyes. "Have you not been taught the history of the Oracle?"

"I wasn't *taught* much of anything. After Stephen found me, he tried to help. As a psychic, he knew about as much about Oracles as I did, but that didn't stop him. He reached out to anyone he could think of to help with my education, but even then, it was mostly trial and error, with an emphasis on the error. Christ, it was such a mess." Gray chuckled, shaking his head.

Dreo frowned. "In times of war, Oracles were always consulted before heading into battle. They would use their skills to determine whether the campaigns would be fruitful or merely an expensive form of population control. The skills of an Oracle were highly coveted and revered. Kingdoms that housed Oracles were considered to be blessed by the gods."

Gray laughed scornfully. "I think I'm living proof that being an Oracle is more curse than gift. My life has been a nightmare."

"It is true that you have been faced with many trials and tribulations. That, I feel, had more to do with the loss of your family and your people, than being cursed. Throughout history, Oracles have always lived in close family units. Even the extended family of an Oracle, while not always having the gift themselves, were welcomed into the community. Their children were sheltered and cherished. They would have assigned you a protector whose sole purpose would have been to guide and protect you. As their numbers began to diminish, they became even more protective of their young." Dreo's expression softened. "I could not even hazard a guess as to how you ended up in the human world, forced to fend for yourself. It is not where you belong."

"Of course, it's where I belong." Gray scowled. "I am human."

Dreo shook his head. "You are no more human than I am. There has never been an Oracle born to wholly human parents."

Gray straightened, his skin going pale. "I don't understand. How am I—then who—?" The pity he saw in Dreo's expression was almost more than Gray could take.

"There have been few combinations of para couplings that have produced an Oracle. Of those that were successful, none have solely involved a human pair. I have heard of a few cases where one of the parents was human but never both." Dreo looked up, his expression thoughtful. "It will take a bit of research to determine where and from whom you were born, but it should be possible." Dreo leaned over him, lifting Gray's chin so they were eye to eye. "Is that something that interests you, Oracle? Would you like to know where you come from?"

Overwhelmed, Gray stared at Dreo in silence, shock robbing him of his voice. It was natural to want to know where you came from. Sadly, he had long ago had to come to grips with the fact that his lineage would always be a mystery. He hadn't had the luxury of such curiosity. It had been more important for him to focus his energy on staying alive and sane. Gray had closed the door on his past. He didn't know how to handle the knowledge that that door wasn't closed as tightly as he'd assumed.

Dreo must have seen the indecision warring in his eyes. Grabbing a handful of Gray's shirt, Dreo dragged him into a tight embrace. His thick, muscled arms banded around Gray's smaller frame, not allowing for any distance between them.

Gray tensed, ready to throw off the oppressive hold and regain his freedom. However, when the heavy weight settled around him, the need to flee didn't take over. Instead, warmth and comfort washed over him. The tension in his body eased as he found himself sinking into the Demon's soothing embrace.

"I apologize, Oracle." Dreo's voice was surprisingly soft. "This is a discussion better saved for a later day, when we have the time to give it the proper focus. For now, accept it as an option tabled for further review, okay?"

Gray nodded his agreement into Dreo's hard chest, without lifting his head. He was becoming entirely too comfortable with this Demon, but there was nothing he could do to stop it. Every minute he spent in the other man's company increased the pull he felt toward him. It was getting harder and harder to fight his attraction. Though he wasn't prepared to admit it, he knew it was pointless to deny the truth any longer—Andreo Demos was his mate.

Gray was surprised when there was no fear or panic inspired by that knowledge. He'd never thought of himself as someone who would settle down and do the whole happily-ever-after thing. Now, it seemed that all he needed was a house with a white picket fence and two point five kids, and he could be a candidate for All-American Family, Gay Edition. He bit back a laugh at the image that burned into his brain. Dreo placed a chaste kiss on Gray's forehead. Lifting his chin, Gray hoped to entice Dreo into something a little less PG rated. The Demon Lord stepped back, an amused grin tugging at his lips.

"While I would like nothing more than to take you back to my room to further demonstrate the benefits of taking a lust Demon for a mate, we have a mission to complete. The sooner we locate the murderer, the sooner I can have you tied to my bed with my cock planted up inside your tight ass."

Gray swallowed back a moan at the image Dreo's words created in his head. He had no problem visualizing Dreo's muscled body draped over his own, sweat slicking his skin as he pumped his massive cock into Gray's hole, stretching him wide. He could practically feel the glorious, burning stretch of his asshole as it worked to accommodate his Demon's member.

Feeling his cock start to respond, Gray knew he needed to get his mind out of the gutter and back to the matter at hand. If he wanted any chance of making his fantasies a reality, they needed to resolve the issue of who murdered the Lord of the Underworld, sooner rather than later. Rolling his shoulders to relieve some of the tension building inside him, Gray released a breath and took a few minutes to get his rampant libido under control. Lifting his gaze, he acknowledged Dreo with a nod.

"Okay. What's the plan?"

"I would like your team to join up with my guards on this one," Dreo responded, authority ringing in his voice. "Whoever tampered with the room is still in the Underworld. We've been on lockdown since the murder. No one in, no one out, with the exception of myself, you and your men. If one of them can pick up a scent from the murderer or his Oracle, we will have a distinct advantage. I don't believe they would have constructed a contingency plan based on the off chance that you would have Shifters as bodyguards. Since a Demon's scenting ability is barely greater than a human's, I don't think they would have thought it necessary to attempt to hide theirs. I would like half of the men focused on that task."

"I'll lead that team," Maddox stated, stepping forward. "These are my men and I've got the best nose of the bunch. If they're still here, we'll find them."

When Dreo looked hesitant, Gray pushed forward. "Great! Now that we've got that settled, what about the other half of the men?"

Dreo shot him a mild glare. "You, my mate, will be providing them with a list of all the Oracles known to work with Demons who would have sufficient power to assist in this kind of task. I agree with your earlier assessment—it will be much easier to draw out the Demon involved if we are able to single out the Oracle. The remaining men will be using your list to track down those Oracles to eliminate them as suspects, or to confirm their involvement."

"And what will you being doing, while we are out tracking down your murderous fiends?" Maddox had his arms crossed over his broad chest and a suspicious glare plastered on his face.

"I have to go speak with the Council. They need to know what happened with Povell and they'll also want an update on our progress finding the murderer. It is never a good idea to keep the Demon Council waiting."

Worry drove Gray forward. "But Povell said they wanted to question you about your involvement in Lucifer's death. That sounds like they think you had something to do with it."

Dreo smiled. "Don't worry about me. Yes, there are maybe a handful of Council members who would like nothing better than to have me blamed for this. If I was found guilty, they could strip me of my power and title and banish me to spend eternity in The Pits."

Gray gasped in outrage, but Dreo covered Gray's lips with his fingers before he could voice his displeasure.

"They are in the minority, my mate. You forget that I am also a member of the Council. I am both older and stronger than any of those who seek to bring me down. They are of little concern to me."

Gray watched him warily. "If you're sure," he muttered, still unconvinced.

"I am," Dreo answered confidently. "I will be back soon. In the meantime, with both Maddox and I occupied with other things, I am assigning Balen as your personal guard until we return." He motioned to the blond Demon, who gave a cocky nod in response. Dreo shook his head in amusement. "Sometimes I forget that he is almost as old as I am. Balen and a few of his men will be with you until Maddox or I return. Until that time, you are to follow his orders and keep yourself out of trouble. Is that understood?"

"Yes, Dad," Gray laughed.

"If you're thinking of trying to keep Gray out of trouble, you might want to try a padded room. Anything short of that and you're just hoping for the best." Of course Maddox chose that moment to swagger over. He put an arm around Gray's shoulder and gave him a good squeeze.

Gasping for breath, Gray gave him an elbow to the ribs followed by a hard pinch to his inner arm. Maddox shrieked like a little girl and bounded away from him with an arm wrapped protectively around his ribs. Gray scowled at his friend. "That's what you get, douche bag. Never forget, smaller doesn't equal weaker."

Maddox rolled his eyes while still nursing his abused ribs. "Yeah, yeah, yeah," he muttered petulantly. "I got it, already. Really, though. Did you have to pinch me so hard?"

"You call yourself a Shifter?" Gray teased. "You're such a baby."

"But you've got those boney little fingers," Maddox whined pitifully.

"If you two are done," Dreo interjected, putting an end to their fun. He turned his attention back to Gray with a serious expression. "Balen has orders to bring you back to my suite when you are done going through the list of possible Oracle suspects. I want you to stay there until I return. My rooms have enchantments preventing uninvited 'guests'. I would feel better knowing you were there, safe."

"What if you need my help catching the murderers?

"Your lone duty in this is to *See*. The others have been trained to handle these types of people. I see no point in having you out chasing down murderers where you might become damaged or upset. Leave the more hands on work to them."

There was silence for a moment before Gray and his guards burst out laughing. Dreo's face darkened, his confusion clear, as the Shifters practically rolled on the floor. Maddox had tears running down his face and was clutching his gut as he tried to get himself back under control.

"Yes," he wheezed, trying to catch his breath, "we would hate to upset Gray's delicate sensibilities." The statement brought on a new round of laughter, which had Dreo shaking his head in bewilderment.

"I don't understand. Where is the joke?" Dreo demanded, irritation seeping into in his voice.

Maddox wiped his eyes and cleared his throat. "When Stephen discovered Gray and realized what he was, he knew he would need protection. He contacted my father and arranged to have him come and stay with the Pack. He's spent the last eight years living with, and being trained by, Shifters." He chuckled. "Gray is no docile lamb. He might be small, but he's scrappy. The only reason he needs to have a protection team is for when he is *Seeing*, or if he has a job that calls for some extra muscle."

Dreo glanced over at Gray who was wearing a smug, if not slightly annoyed, expression. "Well, well, well, Oracle. You have hidden facets. I am glad you are able to protect yourself, but that still doesn't change the fact that I don't see any reason to needlessly put you in danger when we have a group of well-trained professionals who are perfectly capable to taking care of the problem."

Gray glared at him, mouth ajar, ready to dispute his logic. Unfortunately, as he stared into a set of fiery eyes, he couldn't think of a single argument. "Fine," he muttered, gritting his teeth. Moving away, he addressed Maddox and his team. "If you guys need me when you get back, I'll be in Dreo's room, *resting*." Turning on his heel, Gray brushed past Dreo, heading for the door with his team of Demon guards trailing behind him. Reaching for the knob, he paused, turning his attention back to his Demon. "I'll see you soon?"

The smile that bloomed on Dreo's face could have lit the room. "Yes, Oracle. Very soon."

* * * *

Dreo had been gone for hours by the time Gray heard movement outside the suite. He and Balen had spent the time huddled around Balen's laptop, sorting through all the information they could find to narrow down the list of possible Oracle suspects. Balen provided the names and it was Gray's job to recount as much about them as he could. He told them everything he remembered, but with all Oracles' propensity to keep to themselves, there wasn't a lot Gray could tell him. The only information he could really provide was the strength of their gift and their stance on Oracle-Demon relations.

A smile bloomed on Gray's face when he heard the sound of voices from outside the suite. Jumping up, he knocked his chair on its side in his haste to get to the door. Rushing across the room, Gray flipped the lock and jerked open the door. He was ready to give his mate a piece of his mind for keeping him waiting and worried for so long, without a word.

He pulled back in surprise when he realized that the man behind the door, while good looking, was definitely not his mate. The stranger's pale blond hair was so light it was almost white and his gray eyes would have been beautiful if not for the sour expression marring his angular face. Whoever he was, he had to be someone important because he was traveling with his own protective detail. A group of four heavily muscled guards stood around him, armed to the teeth and looking lethal. Surprisingly, none of them looked very happy about being there. It made Gray wonder about the man. If he couldn't even inspire loyalty in his own guards, what did that say for him as a person?

Lost in his own thoughts, it took him a minute to register that the man was speaking to him. By that time, Balen was up from his seat and standing protectively at his side. Something about his face put Gray instantly on guard. It was clear from Balen's expression that he didn't trust their new visitor.

"Are you deaf or just stupid?" the man growled, his mouth twisted into a contemptuous sneer.

Arching a brow, Gray tried to keep his tone neutral while fighting the urge to slam the door in his face. "I'm sorry. Can I help you?"

"Are you the Oracle, Grayson Muir?" The clipped words were practically dripping with distaste. Gray was surprised by his behavior. It was odd for someone to take such an instant dislike to him. For most people, it usually took at least an hour or two in his presence to build up this kind of animosity toward him. Maybe Gray had wronged him in a past life?

"I'm Gray. What can I do for you?"

"You will come with me," he barked, wrapping his fingers around Gray's arm in a vice grip.

"Get your hand off of me, now," Gray ordered. "You don't have the right to put your hands on an Oracle."

Balen surged forward, his face molten in anger. "Release him, Claudis. You know the law. To harm an Oracle is to welcome death."

"That's where you're wrong. Rules regulating the treatment of Oracles are strictly meant to govern the world of humans," Claudis spat. "Here I am, Lord Claudis Xent, member of the Demon Council, and I am ordering Mr Muir to come with me or face charges of sedition."

"And the rest of your council is agreement on this?" Gray asked. From the slight widening of his eyes, Gray knew that this was not a sanctioned confrontation. Whatever Claudis was doing here, it was solely based on his own agenda. Dreo was a member of that same council. No way in hell would he have allowed some half-wit Demon Lord to come and retrieve him. "Where is Lord Demos?"

"Lord Demos is none of your concern. You would do well to focus your energy worrying on your own situation."

"Now you see, that's where you're wrong, Lord Xent," Gray snarked. "Andreo Demos is my mate. He is my only concern. If I find that something has happened to him, I will make sure you regret your actions every day for the rest of your very long life."

Faster than Gray's eyes could register the movement, Claudis had Gray pinned to the wall with his arm wrapped around Gray's neck in a choke hold. Purple flames sparked along Claudis' fingers and hands as the flames licked harmlessly against Gray's protective shields. Irritation sparked in the Demon Lord's eyes. Applying more pressure to his hold, Claudis hunched over Gray's smaller form until his mouth was right at Gray's ear.

"The 'relationship' between you and Lord Demos is over. You are an abomination, Mr Muir, and I will not allow you to pollute the most pure Demon line in history, all because the two of you have convinced yourselves that you are fated Mates. Like stays with like, Oracle. Now, while I may not be able to get away with permanently damaging you, I can damn sure find a nice dark hole to lock you up in. Even abominations like yourself have uses. I believe I will enjoy have my own personal looking glass into the future."

Gray couldn't fight the tremor that rolled through his body. The possibility of being trapped and enslaved had always been one of his greatest fears. It had been a fairly common practice in the past.

Kingdoms that couldn't convince an Oracle to stay with them willingly had often opted to keep one by force. Thankfully, it rarely happened anymore. Still, that knowledge did little to quell his terror at the thought of spending the rest of his life as someone's indentured crystal ball. He'd never survive it. He'd rather die. Sadly, he didn't think Claudis would care one way or the other.

"If you don't get your hands off of him, I will kill you where you stand." Balen's voice was low and deadly, sending shiver down Gray's spine. The complete lack of emotion on the blond Demon's face was unsettling. The vacant calm in Balen's eyes was stalking beast, waiting for the right time to strike.

Claudis' eyes flared with outrage. "I don't take orders from you, soldier."

"But you do take them from the Demon Council. To harm a recognized Mate, is to accept a death sentence."

"I don't need you to tell me about our laws," he spat venomously. "I was there at their inception. I am a Council member... I am above the law."

"Is that so?" Dreo stepped into the room with a contingent of soldiers entering behind him. It was interesting to see that Claudis' own guards were not on alert. They hung back, watching events unfold, but made no move to come to his defense. One even went so far as to nod respectfully to Dreo as he passed. Gray had never been so happy to see Dreo as he was right then. As soon as he locked eyes with his raven-haired Demon, he felt as if a heavy weight had been removed from his chest and he could finally breathe again.

Claudis, on the other hand, looked like he was two seconds from spewing his lunch all over Dreo's hardwood floors. His once handsome face was now pale and pasty. Sweat beaded at his hair line and across his upper lip, giving him a sickly sheen. His eyes were glassy and wide with panic. "Lord Demos," he stammered nervously. "What are you...?"

"It seems that the Council was led to believe that there was a witness who had proof that I was somehow involved in Lord Lucifer's death." Crossing his arms over his chest, Dreo bore down on Claudis, anger clear in the stiffness of his frame and the scowl on his face. "Oddly, even after waiting the required two hours, no witness ever revealed themselves. I have to say, I'm surprised to see you here. I was told you were conducting an interrogation and wouldn't be able to make it to the Council meeting." Walking over to Gray, he wrapped an arm around his shoulder before leaning over to place a gentle kiss on his forehead. Turning back to Claudis, Dreo pinned him with a pointed glare. "Why am I finding you here, harassing my mate?"

Claudis' gaze locked onto Dreo's arm around Gray's shoulder and his expression twisted in disgust. "Mate? You've got to be joking. You are one of only a handful of pure blood Demons in all of the Underworld. The notion that fate would choose this...aberration as your destined Mate is laughable," he sneered. "The Council will never allow it."

Dreo growled and took a step toward Claudis. "This is your one chance to leave here, unharmed. I suggest you take it. If I ever see you anywhere near my mate again, I guarantee you will not get the same chance."

"Very well," Claudis replied haughtily, after a moment's hesitation. "You'll keep your 'pet' on a tight leash, if you know what's good for him. Who knows what could happen to him if he got caught wandering around on his own?" He smirked nastily. "We are in Hell, after all." The threat, while dressed up with pretty words, was there all the same. Without a backward glance, Claudis turned on his heel and practically marched out of the suite. His guards, who had been leaning carelessly against the wall, followed after him at a much more leisurely pace.

Looking up, Gray found Dreo already staring down at him, his dark eyes searching his own. Not for the first time, Gray thought that he could be happy getting lost in those eyes for the rest of his life. Quirking up the corner of his mouth, Gray grinned up at his mate, hoping it might help to break some of the tension in the room.

After a moment, Dreo gave a half-hearted attempt to return the smile. Reaching out a hand to his face, Dreo cupped Gray's cheek in his palm. With the pad of his thumb, Dreo traced the lines of his face, everything from the sharp edge of his cheek bone to the arch of his brow. "So, I see you're making friends." Dreo's tone was mild, but there was a shine of humor in his eyes that sent Gray's heart leaping against his chest.

Giving his mate a blinding smile, Gray shrugged, carelessly. "What can I say? I guess I'm just a people person."

Chapter Nine

Dreo's guards cleared out of the room just a short time later. The door closed quietly behind them, effectively shutting Gray and Dreo away from the rest of the world. It occurred to him, as Dreo excused himself to the bathroom to clean up, that he had spent hours in the suite, pouring over mountains of information, and he had never bothered to spare more than a cursory glance around the space that his mate called home. Wandering about the immaculate suite, Gray finally took a moment to fully explore Dreo's suite. The furnishings were done in deep browns and blues, giving the room an unmistakably masculine feel. Shelves filled with books lined the walls and an enormous bed dominated the center of the room. Examining it, Gray was convinced the massive piece of furniture could, and probably had at one point or another, comfortably sleep at least five fully grown men.

Running a hand along the soft, silky comforter, Gray dared a glance over his shoulder and was met with the most amazing mocha eyes. He felt himself instantly slipping under Dreo's spell. "So," he said with a quirk of his brow, "what's the plan?"

"Rest."

"Rest?" Gray asked dubiously. "Our big plan—the plan that is going to save the Underworld—is rest?"

Dreo smiled patiently. "The other team has been trying to track down the murders by scent for hours. They felt they were getting close, but have remained unsuccessful. They are exhausted. They need time to rest and rejuvenate if they are going to be any good to us tomorrow. We have a few hours before we are supposed to reconvene and continue on with the hunt."

"So, in the meantime," he hedged, "you want me to...rest?" His tone was both curious and hopeful.

"There are many definitions of resting," Dreo replied with a wicked grin. "At some point, I plan on helping you experience all of them. For now, I'm just going to take the edge off." Dreo made a grab for Gray. Cocooning him in his impressive arms, Dreo pulled him in and held him tight against his heart. With Gray thoroughly trapped against his body, Dreo's nimble fingers blazed a trail down his abdomen until they found the closure of his pants. They made quick work of his buckle and zipper. With a jerk, Gray's jeans and briefs were pooled around his feet, and Dreo had a hand wrapped around his thick cock. Giving Gray's dick a few quick pumps, Dreo sank gracefully to his knees.

Gray's eyes widened as Dreo leaned forward and blew a steady stream of hot air over the flushed cap of his cock. When Dreo looked up at him through his inky lashes, Gray's knees went weak and he nearly gave up his load on the spot. His Demon slowly licked a line up his shaft before engulfing the head in the hot, wet cavern of his mouth. Teasing licks flicked around the edge, focusing in on his sensitive glans. Gray cried out, unable to stop himself in the wake of such pleasure.

Without conscious thought, Gray thrust his hips, pushing his cock farther into Dreo's sinful mouth. The Demon carried on, unfazed by Gray's slight act of aggression, his suction increasing with every pump of Gray's lean hips. The sensations Dreo awakened in him had Gray gasping for breath and clinging to the edge of climax. Never before had a lover had him so close to losing control in such a short time.

A telltale tingle worked its way up Gray's spine, signaling his impending release. Not wanting to catch his lover unaware, he grabbed a handful of Dreo's dark locks and tried, unsuccessfully, to pull him off his shaft. Dreo looked up, mouth still full of cock, confusion in his eyes.

"Gonna come—" Gray panted desperately.

Dreo leaned back, his eyes glowing with their inner fire. "Of course." Dreo smirked then proceeded to swallow Gray down to the root in one pass. Gray groaned as Dreo's throat constricted around his dick. No matter how badly he wanted to, Gray knew there was no way he could hold back any longer. Two thrusts later and he was shooting his release into Dreo's waiting mouth while experiencing one of the most explosive climaxes of his life. The room blurred and Gray couldn't focus on anything other than how good he felt and how long it would be until they could do it again.

When he finally ran dry, exhaustion claimed him and his knees buckled. Dreo's strength and quick reflexes were all that saved him from getting up close and personal with the floor. In no hurry to stop his ministrations, Dreo continued to lave and tease the spongy head until he was completely spent. After giving the head one last loving lick, Dreo pulled away, allowing Gray's flaccid cock to slip from between his lips. Dreo rose to his feet, making sure to keep a supporting hand on Gray's shoulder. With his legs still feeling boneless, Gray appreciated the gesture.

Dreo took Gray's hand and led him across the room before placing him in the massive bed that completely dominated the room. Sinking back into the pillowy mattress, Gray closed his eyes as he felt exhaustion sinking in. With his hectic schedule, he never got an overabundance of rest and relaxation. At that moment, Gray felt like he could sleep for a year, and the heavenly bed he was in was the perfect place to make that happen. All he needed to perfect the situation was a certain tall, dark and sexy Demon to snuggle with.

When Dreo didn't join him after a few minutes, Gray opened his eyes and was surprised to see his Demon across the room, attempting to straighten his clothes, not trying to take them off, as Gray would have assumed.

"Aren't you coming to bed?" Though his words were spoken softly, the doubt and confusion behind them came through loud and clear.

Giving him a gentle smile, Dreo crossed the room. "No, my mate. You need to rest and regain your strength." Placing a hand on Gray's head, Dreo ran soothing fingers through his hair. "While I might not have your gift, something tells me that we are going to need you at one-hundred percent when it comes time to deal with the guilty parties."

The words were spoken so calmly, Gray was nearly convinced that Dreo had been unaffected by their earlier love making. Only the massive bulge behind his zipper belayed his words.

"Don't you want me to take care of that for you?" Gray nodded in the direction of Dreo's crotch.

Dreo graced him with a wistful smile. "It can wait. You are what's important right now. You needed a release so you would be able to calm down and regain your focus. Now that we've taken care of that, you need to rest and recharge."

"But—"

Dreo's brows furrowed, his expression turning serious. "I know you haven't had a chance to meet many of the Demons that reside in the Underworld, but the situation down here is getting close to boiling point. There is a limited amount of time that we will be able to keep the Demon population sequestered down here before violence starts to ensue. We are being forced to treat our own people like criminals because of the misdeeds of another. It does not sit well with me. When the time comes, I need you to be able to focus, one-hundred percent, on identifying the murderer so things can get back to normal. Do you understand?"

Gray nodded, feeling properly chastised, no longer able to meet Dreo's eyes. He was embarrassed to admit that he hadn't given any thought to the effect recent events were having on the Demon population. Not only had they lost their leader, but also their freedom. No doubt about it—Gray was officially an asshole.

A finger under his chin forced him to meet eyes filled with understanding. Dreo placed a gentle kiss to Gray's forehead before giving him a stern look.

"My words were not meant to upset you, merely to convey the seriousness of our situation. There is no need for guilt or self-recrimination. You answered our call for help. We will be forever in your debt. Now," he said, straightening to his full height, "you need to rest and I have work to do. I am going to join the teams and assist with tracking down the Oracles. I have posted Balen and a team of guards outside the door to my suite. If you need anything at all, they are at your disposal." With those parting words, Dreo turned and exited the room, closing the door softly behind him.

As silence filled the room, Gray took a minute to wonder how his life had changed so fast. Just a few days ago, he couldn't have imagined working with a Demon, let alone being mated to one. It was funny how much things could change. Now, after getting over his previous prejudice, Gray was fully prepared to claim Dreo as his mate to anyone who dared to question his feelings for the gorgeous Demon. Dreo was strong, compassionate and cared for his people with his whole heart. Gray knew he didn't deserve him, but he was going to keep him anyway. No one had ever accused him of being a good sharer.

As he settled back into the soft cocoon of blankets, the day's events seemed ready to take their toll on him. Gray shuddered as a wave of exhaustion crashed over him. Despite his earlier denials to Dreo, Gray felt his eyes begin to droop and his breathing start to slow. Maybe he would rest his eyes while he waited for Dreo to return—just for a minute. Darkness began to build on the edge of his vision and he knew he was fighting a losing battle. There wasn't anything else for him to do at the moment, and it was getting so hard to keep his eyes open. A little nap might not be a bad idea.

After all, what's the worst that could happen?

* * * *

Gray woke alone and in darkness. Whether it was minutes or hours later, he had no clue, but he instinctively knew Dreo had not returned. Exhaustion weighed heavily on his body. His sleep-muddled brain was questioning what would have caused him to wake, when raised voices, just outside his room, reached his ears. When there was no immediate sense of recognition, Gray's interest spiked.

Groggy and still trying to wipe the sleep from his eyes, he managed to hoist himself out of bed and shuffle over to the bedroom door. He didn't remember Dreo leaving it cracked open, but the beam of light streaming across the floor belayed that thought. As he neared the door, the voices quieted. He was beginning to wonder if whoever it was had left when voices once again filled the air outside his room.

"This is madness. We should have found another way." Deep and rough, the voice was unmistakably male. It triggered something in the back of Gray's mind. He was sure he had heard the voice before, but no matter how hard he tried, he couldn't seem to place it. It figured—he'd always been better with faces. Oh, well. It was probably just one of the guards Dreo had assigned to protect him while he rested.

"There was no other way—you know that." The second voice was higher, more feminine. Gray was sure it was a woman. Another guard? Thinking back, he didn't remember there being any female guards in the group Dreo had had with him.

"This whole situation has been fucked up from the beginning," the man argued. "Nothing has gone the way you said. Maybe we need to take a minute and rethink things. If I could just talk to him—ask him about what happened, then maybe—"

"I told you what happened! Are you questioning my abilities?"

"No! Of course not," the man stammered. "I'm just worried. Andreo Demos is one of the most powerful Demons in the Underworld and he is leading the hunt to find us. It's rumored that he is stronger than even Lord Lucifer. If he wanted to rule, the throne would be his, no questions asked. Add to that the fact that he has an Oracle and Shifters helping him—we are fucked."

"You overestimate Demos and his Oracle," the woman sneered. "Grayson Muir's reputation is mostly hype and good luck. He worked a couple of high profile cases for the police and suddenly he's the most powerful Oracle in the world? I don't think so. I'm ten times the Oracle he could ever hope to be and soon, everyone will know it."

Gray's breath hitched. He couldn't believe what he was hearing. It was clear that whoever was in the other room was responsible for the murder of Lord Lucifer, but why the hell would they be holed up in Dreo's suite and how had they gotten in? Dreo had said he was posting guards outside to keep an eye on things while Gray slept. Did that mean the man was one of Dreo's guards? Anger filled him at the thought that one of Dreo's guards could have betrayed him. From his actions, Gray assumed that Dreo was very close to his guards—even considered them friends. The knowledge that one of those 'friends' may have betrayed him would cut the Demon deeply. Gray made a promise to himself that he would make them pay. No matter how long it took, he would make them suffer for harming his Demon.

When the talk outside his room escalated to bickering, he tuned it out, focusing instead on finding a way out of the room before they realized he wasn't as unconscious as they'd assumed. After a quick inspection, it became very clear that he was screwed. Dreo's bedroom had three doors—one leading to the connecting bathroom, one opening into a massive walk-in closet and the last leading back out into the common area of the suite where he would be treated to the company of admitted murderers.

Plunking down on the bed, Gray strained to think of something—anything—he could do to get himself out of his current situation, but came up with nothing. While being an Oracle did come with amazing powers, those powers could do nothing to help him out of the cluster fuck he now found himself in.

Running his fingers roughly through his hair, Gray huffed out a breath of frustration. He hated feeling helpless. After spending the first half of his life at the mercy of others, he had vowed to never be helpless again. It made his current predicament all the more grating.

If only Dreo were here, he'd know what to do —

With the Demon now center stage in his mind, Gray thought about everything he'd learned about Andreo Demos during their brief time together. While he hadn't known the lust Demon for very long, Gray already felt a connection with him, stronger than anything he'd ever felt before. He no longer had any doubts about the reality of their being mates. Instead of the usual repulsion he felt when faced with a possible relationship, Gray was filled with a sense of peace and joy. The thought of spending the rest of his life tied to Andreo Demos felt like coming home. It was too bad a Demon mating wasn't more like a

Shifter mating. If it was, Gray wouldn't be in his current situation.

When Shifters mated, the bond that formed between them had both physical and mental consequences. Mates grew in strength, bolstered by the added strength of their perfect, fated match. A mental connection also formed, bridging the gap between minds, intertwining thoughts and emotions until they were practically one person.

Gray had always secretly longed for that kind of connection. It was why he had fought so adamantly against getting into a normal relationship. After living with Shifters and witnessing the depth of their connection, accepting anything else seemed like a pale imitation. Gray had looked, but hadn't found a mate in the Shifter community. He had decided he would rather be alone then settle for anything less than the kind of connection they had with their mates.

Sadly, Dreo was not a Shifter. Gray knew nothing about a Demon mating or about what, if any, additional gifts may come with it. Dreo hadn't mentioned anything, so Gray was at a loss. He had to assume they did not come with a similar mental connection, or Dreo would already know that Gray was in trouble and he'd be breaking down the door. That being said, he didn't feel cheated, like he had expected. Dreo's care and concern were more than enough to keep Gray happy for the rest of his life.

A noise near the door had Gray looking up. The possibility that Dreo might have come for him immediately filled Gray with foolish excitement. His heart sank into his stomach when, instead of smoldering mocha eyes, he met an icy-blue gaze filled with anger and resignation.

"Oracle, it's good to see you are awake. There's no need for you to stay hidden away in the bedroom. We've been waiting for you. Please, join us?"

As he stared at the man before him, the recognition was immediate. Gray tried to swallow around the lump in his throat, his mouth suddenly as dry as the Sahara. He licked his lips, desperately searching for a response that wouldn't get him killed faster. Now that he knew the identity of one of the conspirators, Gray had no doubt that his life expectancy rate had just dropped dramatically.

Slowly rising to his feet, Gray smiled wanly. "Of course." He took a few steps toward the door before throwing a cautious look over his shoulder at his captor. "I just have one question."

"Oh? And what would that be, Oracle?"

"Tell me why you would betray Dreo like this. Why, Balen?"

Chapter Ten

"You wouldn't understand," the blond Demon snarled.

"Try me."

"My whole life has been a lie. I couldn't live with it anymore. I had do to something—change something."

"By killing the Lord of the Underworld? Are you out of your mind?"

Balen looked away, but not before Gray caught a glimpse of something that looked a lot like regret on his handsome face. "Lord Lucifer's death was unfortunate. It was an unplanned inconvenience. I just wanted to speak with him—make him admit what he had done. He needed to take responsibility. His death has made that impossible."

"Responsibility for what?"

"For his crime," Balen said simply, a faraway look on his face.

"What was his crime?" Gray probed, confusion warring with his sense of self-preservation. If he could understand the reasoning behind Balen's defection, maybe Gray could convince him to turn himself in to Dreo without any more violence.

Balen watched him, head cocked curiously. "You'd like to know his crime, Oracle? Why don't I show you?"

Before Gray had a chance to process his words, Balen grabbed his wrist in a near-crushing grip. Gray didn't understand his action until he felt his vision start to blur. *What the hell!* It seemed that Balen had picked up a few things from working with an Oracle. Somehow, he had learned how to force a vision and had decided to demonstrate his skill. Whatever Balen wanted Gray to see must have been pretty important to him because forcing a vision took an incredible amount of energy. He had to be desperate to go this route. Questioning the other man's mental status, Gray was sure he didn't want to see anything Balen wanted to show him. Unfortunately, it didn't seem that Gray was going to get a choice.

Gray's vision continued to blur then darken. He waited for the oily sensation that always accompanied his truly horrific visions, but it never came. He was both surprised and relieved. Maybe the vision wouldn't be as bad had he had expected. As his vision went black, Balen's grip gentled slightly but remained firmly around his wrist. The heavy weight was surprisingly comforting in the face of what was to come.

When the images started, Gray was surprised by the normalcy of what he was seeing.

A stunning young woman smiled, her long platinum hair swirling around her as she danced to an unheard melody. The same woman, walking through the streets of the Underworld, arm in arm with a young Lord Lucifer, a shy smile playing on her lips. Lucifer, again embracing the woman before taking her mouth in a passionate kiss. The woman again, this time heavily pregnant, pleading with Lord Lucifer's personal advisor for a chance to speak with the Demon king, only to be forcibly removed by the sneering little man with an order never to return. The woman, her once luminous smile now only a small, tired mockery of what it had once been. She held the hand of a small, beautiful blond boy as they made their way through crowded streets to the small, rundown apartment they called home. And finally, an adult Balen, hunched over the bedside of the woman, her face drawn and pale. No longer the beauty she had once been, she appeared to be wasting away before Gray's eyes. Small hints of the woman she had once been still lingered, making it clear that Balen could be none other than her son. She raised a wasted hand to his face, gently cupping his rugged jaw and graced him with a small smile, an act that seemed to take much more effort than should have been possible. She whispered quiet words of love and regret to the adult Balen. She spoke until both her words and strength failed her. Only then did she finally succumb to the death she had been forced to fight for much too long.

As Gray's vision returned, he was surprised at the wetness on his cheeks. He had learned a long time ago to separate himself from what he was seeing or risk losing himself to the devastation that accompanied most of his visions. The woman's story—her courage and sacrifice—tore through him, becoming a throbbing pain in his chest.

Looking up, Gray met Balen's red-rimmed eyes, the pain in them no longer muted, but fresh and all-consuming in its intensity. Gray wanted to reach out and comfort the man who had loved her and suffered by her side for so long. The man who had once been that sweet, blond-haired boy who'd loved his mother more than anything else in the world. The boy whose greatest wish was that one day, if he tried hard enough — could be good enough — maybe his mother would smile at him, just once, with real joy in her eyes. His greatest sorrow was that he had never seen that dream become a reality.

Gray wanted to wrap that boy in his arms and tell him that it hadn't been his fault. He wanted to explain that sometimes a loss is too great — too consuming — to ever really come back from. Gray wanted to explain to the boy that an evil man, thirsty for power, had played games with his life and destroyed what should have been. Even now, after riding along on the vision, Gray didn't think Balen truly understood what had happened all those years ago to cause so much devastation in the woman he'd loved more than his own life. Emotion and false information clouded his judgment, keeping him from being able to see that he, his mother and even his father had been used as pawns in one man's desperate attempt to gain power.

"Balen," Gray rasped, his throat thick with tears. "I'm so sorry — "

"No!" Balen choked out. His voice had an edge that told Gray the other man was on the verge of losing it. "You don't understand. I don't want to hear that you're sorry. I don't want your pity. I need you to witness his crime. People have to see that the great Lord Lucifer wasn't the man everyone always believed him to be. They need to know what he did to her."

Balen was right. Gray didn't understand. His vision had been heartbreaking, true, but there hadn't been any crime — at least not one that Gray had been aware of. He was just about to tell the Demon as much, when he saw the raw desperation in Balen's eyes. Despite his erratic behavior, it was clear that Balen truly believed what he was saying. In Gray's opinion, that unwavering belief justified another look. Reaching out, he placed a comforting hand on Balen's arm and gave it a squeeze.

"You're going to have to explain it to me, Balen. What is it that I'm supposed to see?"

Balen eyed him warily, as if he was expecting Gray to mock him for his belief. Gray gave him a reassuring smile, hoping the other man could see that he really did want to help him if he could. After a moment's hesitation, Balen's shoulders relaxed marginally and his eyes softened. Gray was going to take it as a good sign.

"What do you know of Demon matings?"

"Honestly, not much. I haven't had a lot of experience with Demons until recently. The only information I know is what Dreo mentioned in passing." Balen watched him expectantly but said nothing. Gray shrugged, confused by the new direction of their conversation. "He just told me was that it was extremely rare for a Demon to find their true mate."

"He told you nothing else?"

Frustrated with Balen's ambiguity, Gray struggled to remember details from his earlier conversation with Dreo. If he was being honest, Gray hadn't really paid that much attention, deeming the information unnecessary since it had nothing to do with him. *Funny how things change*, he thought, chagrined. A flash of memory hit him, then, bringing back more of their conversation, as well as a growing understanding of what Balen was trying to make him see.

"He said that Demons are sterile until they meet their true mate. That's why it's so rare to see a Demon child and why many Demons choose to convert humans. It's the closest many will have to ever having a child of their own." Gray's mind was spinning, his thoughts running in a million different directions, trying to process what he thought he knew until they coalesced into one cohesive thought.

"Lord Lucifer was your mother's true mate."

If Gray had thought his understanding would make Balen happy, he was destined for disappointment. Balen's brows drew together and a frown formed on his lips, marring the normal beauty of his otherwise handsome face. Gray could understand his anger. Balen's mother's love for the Demon Lord had ultimately led to her depression and subsequent death. She hadn't been able to cope with the loss of her mate, holding on long enough for her son to reach adulthood before succumbing to the mercy of death. It was a tragedy.

Gray's mind raced as he digested what he had learned. While he didn't know much about Demon matings, he knew a lot about the bond between Shifter mates and assumed many of the aspects would carry over. Most para matings had a similar core structure. Right away he was struck with a blaring warning sign.

"I don't understand. If they were mates, how was he able to leave your mother? With Shifters, once they meet their mate that's it. They will never love another and it would be impossible for them to leave their mate."

"You understand perfectly," Balen sneered. "Demon matings are not so different from other para matings. As my mother's true mate, Lucifer should never have been able to walk away from her. When Demons mate, there is a blood bond that essentially ties two lives together. It increases the strength of the mated pair, while also making it necessary for mates to stay together or face illness and possible death."

"If that's the case, how did Lord Lucifer manage to stay away from your mother all those years?"

"I don't know," Balen answered solemnly. "It should have been impossible. The only answer I have been able to come up with is that Lucifer had to have found a way to mute or destroy his side of the bond. Otherwise, there would have been no way he could have left my mother without suffering from similar side effects. I've done my research. At the very least, he would have suffered from lethargy, mood swings and a general weakening of his powers. At worst, he would have suffered the same fate as my mother," Balen snarled, anger and loss rolling off him in waves.

Gray pondered Balen's words. No matter how he tried to spin the facts, the situation still didn't make sense to him. Why would a powerful man, the leader of his people, choose to weaken himself rather than claim the woman fate had chosen to be his alone? The simplest answer was—he wouldn't. There would have been no benefit in it and, in Gray's experience, powerful men didn't make decisions where there was no benefit for themselves. That being said, it begged the question—who would have benefitted from Lord Lucifer's weakness?

"Tricky, tricky, tricky," Gray murmured.

"Excuse me?"

Gray jolted, not realizing he had spoken aloud. "Sorry," he stammered, "I was just thinking."

"What were you thinking?" Balen asked skeptically.

"I was thinking—either Lord Lucifer was really stupid, or someone else was very smart."

"What the hell are you talking about?" Balen asked, his irritation clear.

"If Lord Lucifer had become too weak to rule, who would have been next in line for the throne?"

Balen jerked, his expression startled. "Why would that matter? I don't see what that has to do with anything."

"Well, think about it. In your scenario, Lord Lucifer gives up his mate, his child, a chunk of his power and is also suffering physical side effects. Where does it get good for him? I see him losing everything good in his life and getting nothing back in return. Why would anyone do that?" Gray raised a brow in challenge.

"Maybe it wasn't about what he would gain," Balen shot back belligerently. "Maybe he just didn't want to be saddled with a mate and a kid and he was willing to give up anything to get rid of us." It was clear in his tone, not even Balen believed that explanation. That being the case, they were back to Gray's original question—who had the most to gain?

Gray was so busy considering the possibilities that by the time he sensed an additional presence, it was already too late. Gray noticed a displacement in the air behind him a moment before something cold and hard snapped into place around his neck.

Jerking away, he turned and was shocked to find a woman standing behind him. Even more surprising, was the fact that he knew her. With her *café au late* skin, milk-chocolate eyes, and long sheet of honey-brown hair, Opal Vasquez was as gorgeous as usual. She could have been a model with her stunning features, miniscule waist and nearly six-foot height. Unfortunately for the modeling world, being an Oracle was a much more lucrative career choice. While her power level placed her as a mid-level Oracle, she had a great publicist who kept her name in constant circulation. It didn't matter whether it was for her skill as an Oracle, or what married Hollywood actor she was having an affair with—if her name was in print, she considered herself a success and, therefore, was constantly trying to stake her claim over the top spot in the rank of Oracles. She was the Paris Hilton of the Oracle world. While those tactics might mean something to the society circles, those who were looking for an Oracle of value knew to look elsewhere. Sadly, Opal still hadn't learned that notoriety wasn't the same as quality.

"Opal? What are you doing here?" Gray's words slurred together and a wave of lethargy washed over him, nearly driving him to his knees. The object around his neck grew heavier, as he struggled against unconsciousness. Using more effort than should have been necessary, Gray lifted his head and met Opal's gaze, startled by the malicious gleam he saw shining in her eyes.

"Grayson Muir," she purred. "Fancy running into you here. My goodness! You're not looking so hot. Feeling a bit tired? Kind of sluggish? Hmm—I wonder why that would be." Sneering, she lifted her hand to his neck and traced the curving line of the metal wrapped around his throat. It had to be a piece of specialty jewelry, to drain him so quickly. Some kind of spelled necklace or collar. Remembering the click of a lock snapping into place moments earlier, Gray glared at Opal accusingly.

"What have you done, Opal?" With his strength waning fast, his voice was barely more than a whisper.

A wide grin appeared on the woman's face. "Not much. Just taking back something that was supposed to be mine." Tapping the edge of the collar, she scowled at Gray. "You know, you should really stay out of things that don't involve you or your *precious* humans. This whole situation could have been avoided if you'd just stuck to your highbrow principles and refused to work for the Demons. You've got no one to blame but yourself."

Gray's body felt heavy, like it was slowly filling with cement, and he was gradually losing feeling in his limbs. His legs gave out, sending him careening to the floor in a messy pile. Not knowing what she had shot him up with had Gray on the verge of panic.

"I—Oracle—can't h-hurt—" Gray gasped, no longer able to make his voice cooperate.

Opal bent over his prone form, running a deceptively gentle hand through his hair, brushing it back from his face. "Silly, Gray. I'm not going to hurt you—at least, not yet."

Chapter Eleven

At some point, Gray must have finally passed out because when he opened his eyes, he was no longer in Dreo's suite. Instead of the heavy oak beams that crossed Dreo's bedroom ceiling, every inch of his new location was covered, floor to ceiling, in dark river stone. His body shook with tremors, the floor he was lying on was so cold. Gray felt like he was laying a slab of ice. Taking in his surroundings, or lack thereof, it was safe to assume he was in a basement or some other type of underground storage area.

Testing his limbs, he found that although he was a bit stiff, he had regained most of his normal range of motion. His head, on the other hand, was pounding, and his mouth felt like he had swallowed a mouthful of wood chips. Unfortunately, a quick check of his neck showed that he was still wearing his new accessory and the effects of it had given him the worst case of dry mouth he'd ever experienced. He now had one more reason to hate her guts. And to think, he'd always tried to be nice to her and give her the benefit of the doubt, even when everyone else thought she was just a hack.

What a bitch!

As Gray dragged himself to his feet, a wave of dizziness threatened to send him right back down. Thankfully, after closing his eyes and taking a few deep breaths, his equilibrium returned. Pacing around the room, he began trying to coax blood flow back into his extremities while looking for any possible means of escape. He had nearly completed a full circuit, without finding as much as a door or window, when a low moan sounded from the far corner of the room. Shocked to his core, Gray gave a shout and practically jumped out of his skin. With a hand on his chest, he took deep breaths in a desperate attempt to calm his racing heart.

After a few minutes, the pounding in his chest eased back to a more comfortable rhythm. Squinting into the darkness, Gray tried to make out the shape or any features of the room's other inhabitant. Not for the first time, he regretted being born human. If he had been a Shifter, seeing in the dark would be a breeze. As it was, all he could see was a large blob that might, or might not, be another detainee.

Blowing out a frustrated breath, Gray resigned himself to the knowledge that he was going to have to get closer. He needed to know if he was dealing with a friend or foe. Shoring himself up, he brought up an image of Dreo in his mind. He needed his focus to be on living, not on the possibility that whatever was on the other side of the room might kill him in the next twenty seconds.

Not wanting to give himself too much time to think about things and chicken out, Gray put a hand on the cold stone wall and slowly made his way toward the dark shape huddled in the corner. Tiptoeing across the room, he tried to make as little noise as possible. He didn't know what he was sharing a room with, but he was positive that he didn't want to startle it. The closer he got, the more man-shaped the blob appeared. Another moan sounded, this one more pained than the last. This close to the source, Gray was able to pick up on a familiar tone behind the pitiful sound.

No longer afraid, Gray squatted down next to the prone form and pulled back the scratchy wool blanket that had been thrown haphazardly over the figure. With the covering removed, Gray bit back a gasp as Balen's beaten body was put on display before him. The other man didn't appear to be conscious, which, from the looks of his injuries, was a good thing. Someone had thoroughly worked him over, leaving behind a broken, bleeding mass of cuts and bruises. A glint of metal at his neck showed that he, too, was a proud new owner of a necklace from Hell.

Looking down at what was left of the man, Gray was torn between wanting to help and wanting to punch him in his already beaten face for getting them both into their current situation. Luckily for Balen, his conscience chose that moment to kick in. Hunching over the downed man, Gray didn't know where to touch him without causing further damage. If he could wipe away some of the blood, he might get a better idea of what kind of damage the Demon had sustained so Gray could start to treat his wounds. One look at Balen's blanket and Gray knew there was no way in hell he could use it. The scratchy, coarse material would be better used as a torture device than a means to keep warm.

With nothing else at his disposal, Gray grabbed the hem of his shirt and ripped off a long section from the midriff. He had found a small bowl of water during his earlier search, so he began the slow, delicate process of cleaning out and bandaging wounds. With the amount of damage he uncovered, Gray feared he may run out of clothing before he had treated the worst of them. With the extent of his injuries, Gray was surprised the other man had survived his ordeal. He was fairly certain that if Balen hadn't been a Demon, he wouldn't have.

He was cleaning out a particularly deep gash when Balen cried out. His back arched impossible high before his whole body jerked upright. Panting for breath, Balen looked around the room, eyes wide with equal parts confusion and fear. Gray wanted to reassure him but didn't know how his attempt at comfort would be received. The other man had conspired to murder the Lord of the Underworld, after all. Gray should be running in the other direction, not wanting to kiss his boo boos and make him feel better. Regardless, Gray knew he needed to get Balen to calm down. He needed the other man operating at an even keel if they had any hope of escape.

"Balen..." Gray approached the man slowly, not wanting to startle him in his already hyper vigilant state. "What happened to you?"

The tawny-haired Demon startled, as if he was seeing Gray for the first time. "Opal," he rasped, his voice scratchy and raw, his sapphire eyes rimmed in red. "After what you had *Seen*, I knew she hadn't told me the truth—knew we had made a mistake. When I told her that we needed to turn ourselves in, she lost it. She screamed at me—said that there was no way she was going to let the bastard son of a dead Demon ruin her plans. She said that it was finally time to take back what was hers and no one was going to get in her way. I heard a noise behind me, but when I turned to see what it was, someone hit me on the back of the head, then everything went dark. The next thing I know, I'm lying on a cold stone floor, looking up at you."

"Angry, huh? Do you have any idea what Opal was talking about?"

Balen shook his head. "Not a clue. This whole time, I thought she was in this to help me get justice for my mother. Even when she killed Lucifer, I told myself she had done what she thought was right for me. I was a fool."

"Don't be so hard on yourself. Grief makes us do crazy things." Gray rose to his feet and was beginning to turn away when Balen's words clicked in his mind. "Wait! Did you say Opal killed Lord Lucifer?"

"Yes," Balen murmured, his words heavy with regret. "I never wanted Lucifer dead. He was my father, after all. I just needed people to see him for the kind of man he truly was. I wanted him to see the damage his actions had caused my mother—his mate." Balen sighed, wearily running fingers through his already heavily tousled hair.

"When I told Opal that I wouldn't kill Lucifer, she became enraged. She started on about not letting Lucifer get away with what he'd done—that he needed to be punished for what he had taken." Balen looked up and flashed Gray a sheepish smile. "To be honest, I thought she was angry on my behalf. I was flattered that she would care so much about what had happened to my mother and me. Now that I know the truth, I feel like an idiot."

"If you don't mind me asking, how did you even meet Opal? Oracles and Demons don't tend to run in the same circles, if you know what I mean."

Confusion darkened Balen's face. "I've known Opal since she was a child. With her father's position at court, she was around the palace quite a bit when she was growing up."

"Her father is a Demon?" Gray couldn't believe what he was hearing.

Balen gave a slow nod. "As was her mother. Opal is a pureblood Demon — didn't you know?"

Gray shook his head, unable to put his confusion to words. In all the years he'd known Opal, she'd never once mentioned her Demon ancestry. In reality, she had actually been one of the biggest detractors when it came to Demon issues, further encouraging the stereotype of the evil, soul-stealing Demons. While he could understand her not being comfortable broadcasting the information for the whole world to hear, he also couldn't understand her willingness to go to such lengths to disparage her own people. Gray had no idea who his parents were or where they came from, but he couldn't imagine knowingly belittling his own people.

"Are you sure?"

Balen smirked. "Without a doubt. Her father, Vlasik, was Lord Lucifer's personal advisor for virtually one-hundred and fifty years. His passing earlier this year was a great loss to our people."

Opal was a Demon? What the hell?

He was so busy trying to wrap his mind around Balen's news, Gray nearly missed the true importance of his words. "Wait a minute! Did you say Opal's father was your father's advisor?"

Brows pulled together, Balen scowled. "I don't really feel comfortable with that classification."

Gray arched a brow and crossed his arms over his chest. "You're purposely missing the point."

Balen grunted. "Fine. If you want to be technical about it then, yes, Vlasik was *my father's* advisor. Does it matter?"

Did it? Gray wasn't sure. He flashed back to the vision he'd had about Balen's mother and Lord Lucifer. He'd always had total recall of everything he'd *Seen* so the task was easy enough. As the images flashed before his eyes for a second time, something prickled at the back of his mind. There was something there that he was meant to see. He just needed to find it.

He felt like he was on the verge of something important when a noise outside their cell demanded his attention. Silence descended as both men focused their attention outside their small room. For a moment, there was nothing. No movement, no voices, not so much as a breath of air.

Gray was beginning to doubt himself when he heard it again. As he strained his ears toward the sound, he was able to make out the distinctive click clack of shoes on a hard stone floor. He had the unsettling feeling that they were about to have visitors. A quick glance at Balen confirmed the same sense of unease reflected in his eyes. The Demon held a finger to his lips and motioned to Gray, who followed him back into the deep shadows at the farthest corner of the room. While they had no means of escape, they also didn't need to make it easy on their captor. If someone wanted to kill him, Gray was going to make them work for it.

The footsteps stopped right outside their cell, then everything went quiet. Gray began to tremble slightly, his nerves starting to get the best of him. He made himself a promise, then and there, if he got out of this alive, he was going to finally take that vacation Sarah had been harping at him about. It was either that or check himself into a mental hospital, because if things didn't get back to normal soon, he was going to lose it.

"Gentleman, how nice to see you again."

Gray froze, sure that he was trapped inside one of his visions. He couldn't come up with another explanation to make sense of why Povell, a Demon straight from his nightmares, would be standing outside their cell, carefree and unrestrained.

"Po-Povell?"

"In the flesh, my dear Oracle. I just wanted to check and see how the two of you were settling in. I'd hate to think that you weren't enjoying your stay." The smirk on his face and the evil glint in his eyes belayed the truth of his words.

"What are you doing here?" Gray stammered, apprehension settling over him like a heavy weight on his chest.

"Would you believe early release, for good behavior?" Gray just stared at the Demon, too shocked to give an answer. Povell chuckled and shook his head. "Nah, I wouldn't buy it either. Let's just say, I have a friend who's been having a little trouble and called in a favor. Being the good friend that I am, I couldn't bring myself to let her down so — here I am."

"Let me guess — Opal?"

"Look at you, pretty and smart," Povell sneered. "Who would've known?"

Gray scowled but otherwise ignored the Demon's taunts. "Breaking out of Demon jail seems like a pretty risky venture. She must be some friend."

Povell laughed. "Breaking out of jail was the fun part. No, I had other reasons for wanting out of that jail cell and paying off a debt just seemed like good sense. You know, killing two birds with one stone and all that. Clearing my debt with Opal was an added bonus."

"So if helping Opal wasn't the real reason you wanted out of jail, what was the reason?" Gray knew he was going to regret the question as soon as the words left his lips, but by that time, it was too late to do anything about it.

Povell arched a brow as a vicious smile formed on his twisted lips. "My sweet, sweet Oracle, can't you guess?" When Gray didn't answer, Povell released a sinister laugh. "It's you, of course. We have some unfinished business, Grayson Muir. You and your bullshit vision got me thrown in jail, destroyed a friendship I have had for nearly four hundred years and put a permanent stain on my reputation. In case you failed to notice, I am far from pleased," he growled.

"It was your own actions that got you thrown in jail," Gray defended fervently. "My ability to *See* just allowed me to see the true depravity of your crimes and report on them. Your decisions were your own." Povell's expression darkened in response, immediately making Gray wish he possessed some kind of verbal filter. It wasn't smart to piss off a Demon who already wanted you dead, unless your goal was a slow and painful death.

Povell scowled. "I'm not interested in your opinion of my actions. Simply put, your actions and interference have caused me great harm. By Demon law, you owe me a debt, Grayson Muir, and I have come to collect."

Chapter Twelve

Trepidation washed over Gray as he tried to swallow around the now massive lump in his throat. "And what is it you think you're owed as repayment for this supposed debt?" Gray asked, knowing that he was not going to like the answer.

"Just a small thing really—nothing you'll even have a chance to miss. Would you like to guess? No? Well, you're just a kill joy, aren't you?" Povell sighed and shook his head. "Very well. Demon law is pretty basic—a life for a life. You damaged my life—I am going to take yours."

Gray had to fight back a shiver when Povell leveled his icy gaze on him. No way in hell did Gray want Povell to know how much the Demon terrified him. He knew that the small glimpse he'd gotten from his vision was just the tip of the iceberg when it came to the true extent of Povell's crimes. He struggled to keep the emotion off his face, but he could tell by the small smirk forming on the Demon's lips, he hadn't been entirely successful. Gray's teeth began to chatter and his body started to tremble as fear started to dig its claws into him. His knees went weak leaving him struggling to stay upright.

He felt like he was seconds from falling to the floor in a pathetic heap when Balen stepped forward, placing himself between Gray and Povell's malevolent gaze. "You are a fool, Povell. You know as well as I that a criminal is not entitled to a life debt. If you harm Gray, it will be one more crime you are charged with once a new Lord of the Underworld is crowned. I doubt our new Lord will think very kindly of a rogue Demon harming a well-known Oracle who is also the fated Mate of one of the most powerful Demon Lords in history."

Povell smirked. "I guess that depends on who the new Lord is, doesn't it?"

Balen scowled. "I can't imagine anyone powerful enough to become Lord of the Underworld condoning any of the things you've done, least of all an attempt on the life of an Oracle."

"I suppose we'll just have to wait and see," Povell answered cryptically. "As it is, our time together will have to wait, Oracle. At the moment, we are needed elsewhere. Opal has need of your talents and there is still Lord Demos to worry about. I don't want you to worry, though. We will have plenty of time to get acquainted later." Povell smiled lasciviously and blew Gray a noisy kiss before reaching behind his back and producing a large ring of keys. Holding them up, he gave them a good shake for Gray and Balen to see, causing them to clank together, noisily.

"Opal is waiting for us, down the hall. I expect you both to be on your best behavior. The dampening collars you're both wearing should help with that. The spelled metal will keep you from being able to use most of your powers. Even the ones you still have use of will be severely limited. The chance that you would be able to hurt either Opal or myself is very slim but still, it needs saying. If you cannot behave, you will be punished." Lifting his hands, he looked at them briefly before they were blanketed in green fire. Flashing an eerie smile, Povell wiggled his fingers at Gray, causing the fire to dance along the surface of his hands. "Do you understand?" he asked, looking pointedly at Balen.

Gray swallowed and nodded as the memory of being engulfed by those same sickly flames rose up in his mind. While they might not be able to hurt him, he had a feeling Balen would not be so lucky. A glance over at the blond demon showed that while his expression was stoic, he had paled considerably. His eyes widened slightly as he watched the flames flicker across Povell's fingers. With the dampening collars thrown into the mix, Gray had no idea what would happen to Balen if Povell made good on his threat. Not willing to take the change, Gray nodded his agreement.

"Excellent. If you gentlemen will place your hands on top of your heads and exit the cell, we can get this show on the road."

Not seeing that he had any other options at the moment, Gray did as he was directed. He could feel Balen's presence behind him, a small comfort in their current situation. Even with Balen's initial involvement, Gray still felt he could trust the other man. He could even see them becoming friends — if they made it out of this alive, that is. Gray was a big believer in second chances and if anyone deserved one, it was Balen.

Once out of the cell, Povell had them walk ahead of him, directing them through the darkened tunnels of what looked like an old dungeon. There was nothing distinctive on the walls or in the hallway to give Gray any clue where they were being held. His eyes eventually adjusted to the dark and Gray was able make out a faint flickering of light shining out of a doorway at the end of the hall. As they drew closer, the light grew brighter, spilling out into the hall and allowing Gray to make out more of their surroundings.

Near the entryway, Gray noticed a banner hanging on the wall, prominently displaying the black winged insignia of Lucifer's court. Hope filled him at the knowledge that they were still in the palace. Their chances of survival had just risen exponentially. Without knowing how long it had been since he had been taken, Gray was hopeful that Dreo had already discovered he was missing and had sent men out to look for him. His biggest concern now was no longer *if* they would be found. Now his worry was, would they be found in time?

A hard shove from behind sent him careening into Balen who, in turn, nearly took a header into the wall. "Keep moving," Povell barked. "We have a schedule to keep, and Opal doesn't like to be kept waiting."

Oh, no. We wouldn't want to keep Opal waiting, now would we? Gray was tempted to tell Povell that Opal could go fuck herself for all he cared, but he knew it would just encourage Povell to strike out at either Balen or himself. No, he needed to keep his wits about him and wait for an opportunity for escape. If nothing else, he had to find a way to stall Opal and hopefully buy Dreo more time to find them. There was no doubt in his mind that Dreo would come for him. It was just a matter of when he would show.

Another shove reminded him to get moving. Thankfully, he didn't crash into Balen again, but he did wobble on his heels for a moment before Balen's arm shot out to steady him. Gray gave him a grateful smile before he entered the room before him, prepared to face whatever Opal and Povell had in store for them.

The room they stepped into was surprisingly mundane compared to what his mind had conjured up. Instead of the dark, dank torture chamber he'd been expecting, Gray entered a lavish suite, worthy of any five-star hotel. The walls were draped with yards of gold silk and thick, plush rugs were placed strategically around the room. A sitting area had been constructed near the entrance and Gray could just make out the shape of a massive bed in the far corner. Apparently, Opal had discovered an old, abandoned portion of the dungeons and decided to take up residence. It was like a little piece of heaven, smack dab in the bowels of hell. Who knew squatting could be so glamorous? The only things that took away from its glamorous appearance were the piles of old, unused furniture that edged the space. The room must have been used for storage before Opal had taken up residency. It must have been too much work for her to remove the remaining furniture when she was setting up her little haven. Instead, she had merely piled them up near the outskirts of the room.

When Opal stepped forward to meet them, Gray had to bite back a laugh at the irony. If the room was a scene from heaven, Opal had successfully dressed the part of an angel. Her long, dark hair had been brushed to a glossy sheen and hung down her back in fat curls. From the ivory, silk suit and matching pumps, to the fine dusting of shimmer that coated her skin, all Opal needed was a set of downy wings to complete the picture. Only the gleam of madness in her eyes belayed her divine appearance. One look in her eyes and it was easy to see that something evil lived within.

Opal's lips twisted into a sneer as she approached, immediately putting Gray on edge. There was something clearly not right about the woman and he couldn't believe he hadn't recognized it before. His only defense was that he didn't spend a lot of time with any of the other Oracles. Between their initial lack of support when Stephen had gone to them for help with his training and their generally superior attitude, Gray found he had little use for the lot of them. Opal, in particular, had always been one of the most elitist, believing that by being an Oracle she was somehow superior to everyone else. Gray had found her annoying on a good day and did everything in his power to avoid her. As she walked to him with her arms loose at her sides and her shark's smile, he couldn't help but feel like prey.

He saw the muscles of her arms flex, but it was too late to do anything about it when she hauled off and coldcocked him right in the jaw. The force of the blow drove him back a step, but he stayed on his feet. He wasn't willing to let the bitch put him on the ground, at least not without a good fight. When she lifted her hand again, Gray flinched, ready for another blow to land, but it never happened. Instead, she placed her palm on Gray's cheek, giving it a few sharp slaps.

"Gray," she hummed. "It's so good to see you. It's been too long."

"Not long enough," Gray muttered under his breath as she removed her hand from his face.

An expression of mock hurt darkened her face. "Don't be like that. I thought we were friends?"

"Friends don't lock away their other friends' powers and kidnap each other. That type of behavior is usually frowned upon in most circles. As is murder and treason."

Opal took a step back, giving Gray a vicious smile. "Grayson Muir, always such a fine, upstanding citizen. Never one to step out of line or push the limits of the law. I've always respected that about you. It's made you predictable and easy to avoid. If you had just remained true to your convictions and stayed clear of the Demons, you could have avoided this whole messy business."

"You know me, Opal. I've always been a sucker for a good sob story. Dreo made a good case for my help and I couldn't resist. What I don't get is why you would have done this? I've never known you to be one to get your hands dirty. Why now?"

Opal smiled, but it was far from pleasant. "Long ago, Lucifer took something that didn't belong to him. It's been a long time coming, but it's finally time to take it back."

"What could Lord Lucifer possibly have taken that would justify taking his life?"

"Rule of the Underworld, of course." Opal gave Gray a look like she was questioning his intelligence.

"I don't understand."

Opal huffed in irritation. "Before Lucifer's reign, leadership of the Underworld had been passed down in my family for generations. Because of my family's reputation, they were seldom challenged when it came time to reassign leadership. When my grandfather died, my father had been prepared to take over the rule. However, before he could receive the crown, Lucifer stepped in and challenged him." Opal sneered contemptuously. "By some twist of fate, Lucifer managed to defeat my father in combat and took the crown, and leadership of the Underworld, as his own."

"Okay," Gray drawled, "I still don't get what Lucifer took from you. It sounds like he took over leadership of the Underworld through legitimate means—"

"No!" Opal's shriek could have shattered glass. "He stole the crown. Somehow he managed to rig the challenge between my father and himself. My family was always meant to rule the Underworld."

"But Dreo told me that rule of the Underworld was based on strength, not lineage. That being the case, it sounds like your father wasn't strong enough to rule."

A loud crack sounded and then a blast of heat burned across Gray's right cheek where Opal's hand had come in contact with his face. When the pain registered, it was clear that she hadn't held back, her Demon strength in full force. Combined with the deep ache from the previous hit, it was excruciating. It radiated out from his cheek bone in an endless, throbbing wave of pain. Gray was worried that she may have fractured something in his face. Gritting his teeth against the agony, he fought the urge to cradle his cheek, not wanting Opal to have the satisfaction of knowing she had truly hurt him.

"My father was a great man," she snarled. "He would have been ten times the leader that Lucifer was. All he needed was the chance to prove it."

"Wait a minute."

The surprise of Balen's voice had Gray nearly pissing himself. The blond Demon had been quiet for so long, Gray had almost forgotten he was there.

"If you father had challenged Lucifer to be Lord of the Underworld, how did he become the man's personal advisor? That's not a position someone would trust to an enemy."

Opal's answering smile was triumphant. "Demons live forever, dear Balen, or did you forget? My father had nothing but time to work his way back into Lucifer's good graces. It took him almost one hundred years, but he finally managed to convince that counterfeit king, Lucifer, that he had no further designs on the throne. He spent that time planning his revenge. One hundred years spent working out every facet of a plan that would not only allow our family to reclaim what was taken from us, but also destroy the usurper who'd thought to reach above his station. Do you get it now, Balen," she sneered, "or do you need me to draw you pictures?"

"Be careful how you speak to me, Opal," Balen snarled. "I passed my first century of life before you were even a twinkle in your parents' eyes. If either of us needs a refresher on what it means to be a Demon, let me assure you, it is not me." The pointed glare he gave her left little doubt of the contempt he felt for her.

"Poor, Balen," Opal mocked. "So bitter. So angry, and all because dear old dad walked out on your mother." A slow smile formed on her face, but there was nothing pleasant about it. It reminded Gray of the way a hyena would look right before it went for the throat of its downed prey. He watched her cautiously out of the corner of his eye, his muscles bunched and tight as he waited for her inevitable attack.

"Didn't you even bother to question why he left?" she asked, a smirk twisting her lips and malice darkening her features. "I mean, really. For you to have been conceived, Lucifer and your mother had to have been true mates. Have you ever heard of true mates leaving each other by any means other than death? Could you actually be that stupid?"

With his brows drawn, a look of anger and confusion darkened Balen's face. His jaw clenched as he tried to come to terms with what she had said to him. Meanwhile, Opal was watching him with a sickening expression of anticipation. While Gray didn't know much about Demons or their culture, even he could tell that there was an attack attached to the information she had just given Balen. It was just a matter of when the first strike would make contact.

Balen seemed lost. With his eyes narrowed and unfocused, it was clear his concentration was directed inward. Then, everything changed. It happened so fast that if Gray hadn't been watching Balen, he would have missed it.

"You," Balen growled. "You fucking bitch! You knew. All this time, you let me believe my father was a bastard who abandoned his pregnant mate while he ran off to pursue his desire to rule the Underworld. You let me believe the worst of him, knowing it wasn't true." If a look could kill, Gray was sure Opal would have been incinerated on the spot. Balen clenched his fists, taking a step toward the rogue Oracle. "You were right before. There truly is no way a mated couple would voluntarily separate from each other. As they were indeed separated for nearly fifty years before my mother finally succumbed to her sorrow, there has to be an explanation and something tells me that your family was behind it. So the question is—what the hell did your family do to my parents?"

Chapter Thirteen

Opal threw her head back and laughed. The sound was deep and throaty, echoing around the room. It would have been a nice sound if Gray didn't already know what the cause of her joy was. Instead, it grated in his ears like nails down a chalk board.

"Oh, Balen. I knew you weren't just a pretty face. Not too quick on the uptake, but you get there eventually. Not like your father at all." Opal shook her head pityingly and clucked her tongue. "Now that man was a perfect example of brawn over brains. Too dumb to see what was right in front of his eyes."

Balen snarled and advanced on Opal, rage and pain in equal parts flaring in his eyes. Those pale orbs, no longer icy, were glinting with barely contained blue flame. It shouldn't have been possible. Apparently, the dampening collars they had been given weren't quite as potent as they advertised. Now that he was aware of it, Gray could also feel the renewal of his own strength. It was by no means full power, but it was better than what he'd had an hour ago. Hopefully Opal and Povell would be too busy gloating about their superiority to notice that he and Balen weren't quite as helpless as they thought. If Opal made it through this alive, she should definitely consider contacting the manufacturer. While Gray had previously seen the same fire burning in Dreo's eyes and had found the effect beautiful, Balen's inner fire did not encourage the same response. As the pale-blue flame snapped and sparked in Balen's eyes, Gray felt a knot of fear unfurl in his stomach. The anger building in Balen could be dangerous. When released, that kind of mindless rage didn't differentiate between friend and foe. Its sole purpose was destruction.

Gray had no intention of dying anytime soon, especially not when he was so close to having his dream of a family of his own realized with Dreo. Gray knew he reasons might be selfish, but he had never been one to lie or hide his true feelings to appease others. All he wanted was some peace and quiet and his mate's hot, naked body riding him hard. For everything he had done to help those around him, he figured he had earned some time to enjoy his mate and, damn it, he was going to get it even if he had to kill everyone else in this godforsaken room to get it. He was at his wit's end with all this Demon drama. At this point, he was willing to foot the bill to build them a giant cage and let them go all death match on each other—winner takes all. It would certainly make things easier for him.

Balen's brows furrowed and his teeth were clenched. The Demon looked like he was on the verge of attack. Gray took a slow, cautious step back, not wanting to draw either combatant's attention. With as fast as the situation was escalating, he didn't want to get caught in the crossfire.

"This is the last time I ask you, Opal. I am not opposed to beating the answer out of you if I have to. In fact, at this point, I would prefer it. Now, what the hell did your people do?" His tone was hard, dripping with menace and brooking no argument.

Opal openly watched Balen, her brow arched and a considering expression on her face. Lifting a hand, she gently tapped her chin. Gray might have believed she was considering her options if he hadn't caught the conniving glint in her eyes. He knew then, there was no way the situation would end well. They would be lucky if any of them walked away alive.

A slight movement off to Gray's right stole his attention away from the combatants and had him looking around for its source. While Opal and Balen had been causing a scene, Gray had nearly forgotten that it hadn't been just the three of them in that room. He received a harsh reminder when a quick look over his shoulder showed Povell standing directly behind him, an ominous presence at his back. Gray had no idea how the man had crossed the room unnoticed, but the fact that he had did nothing to calm Gray's already frazzled nerves. Neither did the unsettling smile that quirked his thin lips.

"Balen?" Gray hated the sound of desperation in his voice, but he didn't trust the look on Povell's face. He knew his only chance was to stick with the Demon he knew. Hopefully Balen wasn't so lost in his rage that he'd forgotten about Gray's presence. Gray had no illusions about Balen's chance of survival if he allowed something to happen to Gray and Dreo found out. When Gray didn't get a response, he tried again, putting all his fear and annoyance behind the words. "Balen!"

Balen jolted like he'd been struck by lightning, his eyes immediately seeking out Gray. As soon as Gray made eye contact, he realized his mistake. Rage burned in the depths of those twin orbs. Balen's pale eyes were now crackling with eerie blue flames that looked like they were mere moments away from leaving his eyes and setting the room ablaze. For a moment, with that terrifying gaze locked on him, Gray was afraid. There was no recognition in the other man's gaze and Gray had no doubt that Balen was perfectly capable of incinerating them all within seconds. He tried to comfort himself with the knowledge that if Balen did lose control, at least his death would be quick and nearly painless. It would a better death than the one Povell had planned for him.

For just a moment, with his fear pushing at him hard, Gray allowed himself to think of Dreo. He ached for his Demon's touch—longed for the comfort of his presence. Gray had no doubt that as long as Dreo was with him, he had nothing to fear. If only his Demon mate was with him now. Sorrow made an attempt to overtake him, as he thought of how little time they had had together. Gray hadn't realized, until that very moment, how much he had been looking forward to spending eternity with his bossy Demon mate. He wished he'd never been so afraid of what had been building between them. If he'd been braver, he wouldn't have been holding back and he would have told Dreo how he felt. He would have told his Demon that he loved him, because it was true and the man deserved to know. He had a feeling that Dreo, like Gray himself, didn't have a lot of experience with affection that didn't come with strings attached. The words would have meant a lot to him. Gray didn't know how it had happened so fast, but it had, and he didn't regret it. It didn't matter that he hadn't known the Demon for more than a few days. He would cherish that time for the rest of his life—which sadly enough seemed would be coming to an end pretty quickly based on the general feeling in the room.

Turning his attention back to Opal, Balen glared at her with eyes, completely empty of emotion. "What is your answer?"

Balen's words were as much as threat as they were a question. The room had begun to heat as the man's anger built. Gray had already begun to sweat and knew it was only going to get worse if Opal didn't give Balen the answer he wanted.

"Hmm," Opal replied coyly. "You know—I don't think that I owe you any answers. As the daughter of Vlasik Lazarios, the true Lord of the Underworld, I don't take orders from the bastard son of an interloper. If you'll pardon the obvious pun, go to Hell!"

Opal was no longer trying to hold onto her wholesome, innocent appearance and the difference was impossible to ignore. The glow that had seemed to emanate from her was gone. Now, the air around her became heavy and fetid, as if the evil within her was causing her to rot from the inside out. Her sheet of glossy hair now hung in oily, gnarled clumps around her sallow, emaciated face. No longer angelic, she now looked more like something that had crawled into a swamp and died. Gray took a reflexive step back before remembering that Povell was there, just waiting for his chance to strike.

Her transformation elicited a hiss from Balen. "Witchling," he snarled, baring his teeth.

Witchling? Gray had a vague understanding of the term from his studies with Stephen. It was used as a general description for any para who also took up the study of the dark arts. It was considered a universal taboo for any para to study black magic. Magic, combined with their natural para abilities, had unknown and often disastrous consequences. Written accounts, detailing the lives of those unfortunate paras, were very scarce. In most cases, those who attempted it allowed their ambition to drive them into committing unspeakable acts. The cautionary tales gave voice to both the rise and ultimate destruction of the men and women in question.

Armed with that knowledge, Opal's wasted appearance suddenly made sense. Based on the stories, while the dark arts boosted your power base, it was not a gift freely given. It demanded a hefty price. While outwardly it gave the user unnatural powers and strength, internally it corrupted and consumed, destroying everything in its path until the practitioner was nothing but an empty, withered husk. Black magic use explained how she, a mid-level Oracle, had managed to murder one of the most powerful Demon Lords in known history. It also explained how she had managed to block Gray's ability to *See*. If his suspicions were right, Opal had been blocking him for weeks — blocking him, and so much more.

Gray had been born with power. He had never asked for it, but it had always been there, just the same. It had been his constant companion. He'd never know what it would be like to live without it. Nor would he ever experience how desperate some would be to have it. Maybe that was the reason he couldn't imagine what would make someone risk such a fate, all for the sake of power. Just the thought of such a fate had Gray fighting off a shiver of horror.

Dread unfurled in his stomach as his mind began racing through the possibilities. How far had Opal's thirst for power taken her? What other monstrous acts had she been a part of on her rise to the top? Gray had no doubt that Opal would never willingly give them the answers they were looking for. Even under threat of death, she would hold her secrets close, thrilled in the knowledge that closure would forever be beyond their reach. Curiosity had always been his downfall and, with that being the case, Gray knew he had just one option.

Leaning forward, Gray reached out and caught Opal's arm in a steely grip. She jerked at the contact, surprise and irritation clear on her face from the raised brow and snarl tugging at her upper lip. Anticipating her actions, Gray tightened his hold, not allowing her the freedom to pull away. Realizing she couldn't escape, Opal gave him a withering glare.

"Seriously, Gray?" She looked pointedly at his hand on her arm. "What do you think this is going to accomplish?"

Gray smiled as his vision dimmed and began to blur around the edges. "You know me, Opal. I've just got to know."

It was a little known fact that the only way around *Sight Blindness* was direct touch of the person who instigated the block. That, added to Opal's strong bond with her father gave Gray the connection he needed to maneuver around her block and get to the answers they needed. It was a risk he had to take if they wanted to have any chance of stopping her. They needed to know what she was planning. Opal had made a mistake, underestimating him, and Gray wasn't above taking advantage. She was a fool for allowing Gray so close and she was about to regret that mistake. She should have done her research. He knew it was a risk. It broke nearly every rule he had ever set for himself when it came to his *Sight*. He also knew that chances were good that Opal was not going to make it through this night. If she was killed, most of her secrets would go with her. No one knew how many other people out there who were victims of the black widow before him. The potential risk was worth the potential benefit. Dreo might not agree, but he wasn't there to weigh in.

Realization hit her like a bitch slap to the face. She began to struggle in earnest, but it was too late. He could already feel his *Sight* rising up within him. They were past the point of no return and now there was nothing either of them could do to stop the vision to come. Reaching out his other hand, Gray met Balen's angry gaze.

"I think you're gonna want to see this."

Balen watched him, the fire starting to ebb in his eyes. Once extinguished, confusion replaced his anger. He reached out, hesitantly, watching Gray's hand like it was a cobra about to strike.

"It's now or never, Balen." Gray's vision went black as his powers prepared to take him on a ride. His stomach lurched, and Gray knew his time was up.

"Balen! Now!"

Chapter Fourteen

What Gray saw wasn't at all what he had expected. It was so much more. Vlasik Lazarios' revenge had been long planned and all encompassing. Image after image of betrayal flashed through Gray's mind. His heart truly went out to Balen.

Lord Lucifer's destruction had not been quick or painless. Opal's father had wanted to make the leader of the Underworld suffer as much as possible, and he had succeeded. Over his years of service, he had managed to strip the great man of everything he'd held most dear. As Gray watched the scenes flash before his eyes, he felt wetness on his cheeks but could do nothing to reign in his sorrow under the onslaught of treachery. From what Gray could tell, the jealousy Opal's father had had for Lucifer hadn't started when he took over as Lord of the Underworld, but had been going on since their childhood.

A young Vlasik on the streets of the Underworld, watching with envy as an equally young Lucifer enjoyed an outing with his family. A school-aged Lucifer receiving an award for his academics while Vlasik glowered at the back of the room. Lucifer at university, laughing and surrounded by friends while Vlasik stood alone, in the shadows. An adult Lucifer accepting a position on the Demon Council as its youngest member in history, while Vlasik remained a low level Demon. Lucifer and Vlasik, competing in the trials for Lord of the Underworld, after the death of the previous Lord. Lucifer's coronation –

As the images continued to change, Gray started to feel overwhelmed. He'd never used his gifts to this extent before, and was able to admit, he hadn't been prepared for the strain of it. He should have taken a moment to think. Most of his clients just needed him to look at a particular period of their lives, usually needing to see no more than a few years at a time. Demons lived such long lives. There was so much more to see and Gray was starting to suffer under the deluge. As the barrage of images continued, Gray felt his strength begin to wane. Hopefully they could make it to more recent events before he passed out. He'd hate to think it had all been for nothing.

Lucifer holding court before droves of Demons while Vlasik glowered at the back of the room. Vlasik looking on as Lucifer handed down punishment for those who broke their laws. Vlasik following Lucifer through the streets of the Underworld as he enjoyed an evening out on the town with a very familiar blue-eyed, blonde. Vlasik's rage in response to Lucifer's joy when the same blonde told him she was carrying his child –

The images suddenly took a darker cast, as if the reality of a child was the more than Vlasik could take – a line in the sand, never to be crossed.

Vlasik again, this time pouring over an old tome in a darkened room, a symbol of dark magic gracing its cover. Whispered words, a spell, designed to dampen what couldn't be destroyed and in the process, slowly eroded the most important thing in Lucifer's life. The blonde, Balen's mother, heavily pregnant and desperately attempting to see Lucifer, only to be turned away by a sneering Vlasik, who passed along words of indifference and rejection –

The images kept changing, but Gray was no longer paying attention. Something had clicked for him with that last vision and he didn't need to see any more. In a horrible, traitorous way, it all made sense. Gray wanted to weep for Balen and his parents. The injustice of what had happened to them was unthinkable. Gray wished he had the power to turn back time and change what had happened. Sadly, his talents lay only in witnessing the past, not rewriting it. That didn't mean he couldn't at least try to get justice for them, now. Better late, than never.

"Your father did all this?" Gray already knew the answer, but he wanted to see what Opal had to say. He needed to know how deep her involvement ran before he acted.

"Of course," she sneered. "Lucifer made a mistake when he took the crown. Rule of the Underworld was never meant to be his. It was a position well above his station." Opal's lips rose in a mockery of a smile. "Lucifer needed to learn a lesson. He took something that was important to my father. My father just returned the favor."

"And where is your father these days?"

Opal's smile faltered as an expression akin to sorrow darkened her face. "Father died six months ago. My deepest regret is that he never got to see his dream come to fruition. No matter," she said with a shake of her head. "His dream is alive in me and I won't rest until I see it to completion." Her expression was fierce, leaving Gray fighting the urge to take a discreet step back.

"Lucifer's dead. Doesn't that mean you've already completed Vlasik's wish?"

Opal grinned. "Lucifer's death was just a stepping stone—a bonus. My sights are set much higher than that. All the way to the top."

Gray eyed Opal cautiously. "Queen of the Underworld?"

"It's what father would have wanted," Opal replied with a shrug.

Gray didn't think that Vlasik Lazarios had given one second of thought to the possibility of his daughter taking the throne. From what Gray had seen of the man in his vision, the only person he had any concern for was himself. He stayed silent. Let Opal keep her illusions if they made her feel better about what she had done to get where she was. They wouldn't do her a bit of good in the long run.

"Well, it sounds like you've got everything figured out. What do you need me for?"

Opal tapped her chin thoughtfully. "I'm in need of a little...guidance." Sighing at Gray's raised brow, she narrowed her eyes, irritation practically oozing from her pores. "You know as well as I do that we aren't able to use our abilities to see our own futures. Even events with a loose connection are fuzzy at best. I need your skills to help me set my course. Everything has to be perfect! Killing Lucifer was just the first step. To get to the throne, there are many more that will have to be removed from my path. There are others who will try to take what's mine and you are going to help me make sure that doesn't happen. I will gain control of the Underworld and you're going to help me. Understand?"

Great. They were back to the whole imprisoning the Oracle thing again. What was the deal with these

Demons? "If I agree to help you, will you let Balen go?" Gray knew Balen wasn't going to be happy with the question, but Gray had to do anything he could to take of the man who had helped to keep him safe.

Opal's gaze flicked to Balen for a moment before focusing back in on Gray. "Unfortunately, that's not going to be possible. Balen is the son of Lord Lucifer. I won't have him haunting my steps, waiting for the time to take my throne. No," she said, smiling malevolently. "He will be the first to go."

Gray stayed silent as Opal turned and stormed around the room, cursing and mumbling to herself. With a wary eye, he looked on as she flailed her arms, knocking over a lamp and sending a decanter crashing to the floor. Her actions and appearance further proved that her black magic use had already started to eat away at her. Because of black magic's destructive nature, it would eventually start to cannibalize the user's mind, literally driving them crazy. Despite the woman's total loss of sanity, Gray had to admit that her plan was solid. If he were set on world domination, having an Oracle in his back pocket would be a smart choice. What better way to ensure that you get the outcome you want, then to have someone by your side, directing your steps and leading you straight for the path of success? His fear was what would be in store for the rest of the world once Opal got the power and position she sought?

Balen had been suspiciously quiet during Gray and Opal's interaction. After what they had seen in his vision, Gray was becoming concerned. Flicking a glance over his shoulder, Gray found the other man standing stock still, his face a cold mask of fury. A flicker of movement had Gray's eyes zero in on Balen's hands. Small sparks were flaring across his fingertips. The pulsing wave of hellfire grew stronger with every pass. He found himself fighting the instinctive urge to take a step back, desperate to distance himself from the impending storm that was sure to accompany that kind of anger. Unfortunately, the reminder of Povell's presence at his back forced him to keep his feet firmly planted where he was. Opal had obviously been too wrapped up in her plotting to notice the silent rage building in the other man. She had made the mistake of assuming the collars would be enough to hold them indefinitely. Opal would have been smarter if she had just killed them both out right. Now it was too late. Her time had run out, and she didn't even know it.

"Bitch."

The word was spoken so quietly, Gray thought he'd imagined it.

"Fucking bitch!"

No ignoring that. Balen was on the move. His fingers sparked one last time, before hellfire erupted from his hands. With his arms and hands completely encased in blue flame and fury burning in his eyes, the blond Demon made a move toward Opal. Unfortunately, stealth didn't seem to be part of his attack plan. Balen didn't make it more than five feet before Opal noticed his approach. She turned to face him, a venomous smirk on her face.

"Is this the part where we fight to the death so you can avenge your dead parents?"

Balen's enraged snarl was all the answer she got. Not giving her a chance to make the first move, Balen launched himself at her, throwing bolts of blue flame as he moved. Balen's accuracy was seriously diminished under the force of his anger. Most of the bolts missed her entirely, but one shot managed to fly true, striking her in the shoulder and sending her careening into the nearest wall before crumpling to the floor.

With Opal down, Gray had a smidgeon of hope that she might see the futility of this fight and surrender. If one of them didn't back down, someone was going to get seriously hurt and he had a pretty good idea that person was going to end up being him. As the only non-Demon in the room, Gray didn't like his odds of survival if it came to a full-on Demon battle.

Gray's hope didn't last long. As Opal rose, the smile on her face told Gray all he needed to know. Her pleasure at the thought of killing them both just confirmed the knowledge that she would never back down. Opal was willing to risk death for a chance at the crown and she wasn't going to settle. She was running balls to the wall, no holding back.

"Nice shot!" Opal laughed. "Now, I want your honest opinion. What do you think of this?"

Gray didn't have a chance to even process her words before a volley of flaming projectiles were headed in their direction. The small orbs were each about the size of a softball, made entirely of dark purple flame, and were shot in rapid succession, similar to machine gun fire.

If it had been Gray, on his own, facing down such a barrage, he wouldn't have stood a chance. While the shots couldn't have killed him, the residual pain from deflecting them would have been excruciating while also leaving him open for further attack. Thankfully, that wasn't the case. Even with so much anger and rage still coursing through him, Balen didn't falter when he put himself between Gray's body and Opal, using his body as a living shield. While his bulky mass was able to block the worst of the attack, some of the orbs were able to avoid interception and continue on, true to their course.

Gray did his best to avoid the incoming projectiles, but without Demon speed and strength, he was at a distinct disadvantage. He took a hit to his left shoulder and another to the stomach, on the same side. While his natural shields were still in place and kept him from suffering real damage, they did nothing to dampen the pain or driving force of impact. Gray likened it to wearing a bulletproof vest. Its purpose was to save your life—nothing more, nothing less. The hit to the shoulder stung but was manageable. The hit to the stomach, however, was so much worse. The air was driven from his lungs, and the pain was like nothing Gray had ever felt before. He felt like he had taken a wrecking ball to his chest. It didn't help that the force of the impact threw him back nearly twenty feet, leaving him a crumpled heap on the floor, unable to move and gasping for breath.

Huddled in an agony-filled ball, Gray waited for another blow but none came. Cracking open an eye, he watched Balen and Opal locked in combat across the room. In their thirst to destroy each other, they seemed to have forgotten all about him, and Gray was okay with that. He was wholly unequipped to participate this fight. Better to let the Demons duke it out and pray that Balen was the victor. He was having a hard enough time getting air back into his lungs, let alone trying to be an active participant in the fight raging across the room.

"Well, well, Oracle. It seems our time has come at last."

Gray's heart seized. *Povell. How the hell did I forget about that nut job?* A shadow fell over him as a hand wrapped around his arm, jerking him roughly to his feet. The combination of malicious glee and arousal on Povell's face turned Gray's stomach and had him fighting off a shiver of revulsion.

"What you saw in your vision doesn't even compare to what I have planned for you," Povell murmured, leaning in to lick a trail up the lobe of Gray's ear. "That was amateur. This—this will be a masterpiece." Povell closed his eyes and groaned, a look of pure bliss lighting his face. If Gray didn't know the man was imagining Gray's own torture and probable death, he would have said the expression was beautiful. Instead, it just furthered his belief that Povell was an evil, twisted monster that needed to be put down. His death would be a gift to the world.

Gray watched Povell warily, as he walked a slow circle around him. He gave himself a lot of credit for not flinching when the Demon ran a questing hand across the expanse of his chest, around the curve of his waist, before tracing a line down his back and over the cleft of his ass. He barely bit back the whimper of fear that tried to escape when Povell pushed in firmly on the seam of his pants, directly over his entrance. Gray had to fight the urge to throw off his hand and run. Povell's touch made his skin crawl and itch, like being covered in thousands of biting ants. It felt wrong to allow it—made him feel dirty. The only person who had the right to touch him this way was Dreo. Gray belonged to him. No one had the right to touch what belonged to Andreo Demos.

As if that thought had conjured him into existence, Dreo burst through the door, followed by a small contingent of soldiers. With his long hair pulled back in a queue, his jaw clenched and his eyes flashing black fire, Dreo looked fierce. He was every bit the warrior and as far as Gray was concerned, the man had never looked more gorgeous. A combination of Demon warriors and Gray's guards spread out behind him. They stood together, weapons and powers at the ready, and Dreo standing front and center.

"Well, well, well—if it isn't *Lord Demos*, come to grace us with his presence? To what do we owe this pleasure?" Povell sneered, pulling Gray in until his back was pressed firmly against Povell's front.

Dreo growled. "You have something of mine—I want it back."

Povell laughed, squeezing Gray tighter against him. Running a hand down Gray's body, Povell groped him suggestively, eliciting another growl from Dreo. "Oh, you mean the Oracle, here? You must be mistaken. This is my Oracle. I have exciting plans for him," he taunted. "Maybe you'd like to join us? See how it's really done?"

"I am warning you now, Povell," Dreo rumbled, onyx flame flickering in his eyes. "Anything you touch him with, I will cut off before I grant you the mercy of death. Do not test me on this. I will not be giving second chances."

"Oh, yeah?" Povell smirked. Reaching around, he dropped his hand to Gray's groin and squeezed him painfully tight. Gray cried out, the pain intense and nauseating. Povell laughed. "You mean if I touch him like this?"

Dreo's roar was earth shattering. Glass objects groaned from the strain of withstanding the sound and anything metal rattled in its casings. Without any further warning, Dreo launched himself at Povell, murder clear in his eyes. Povell's answering shout was triumphant. Giving Gray a hard shove, he forced him to the ground before turning to face Dreo, green fire already traveling down his arms.

Gray looked on helplessly as the two Demons faced off. The fire encompassing Povell's arms flared brighter as he began to throw bolt after bolt of living flame. As they closed the space between Povell and Dreo, the bolts began to burn brighter, as if they were gearing up to do the most damage possible.

When Dreo didn't so much as raise his hands to defend himself, Gray started to worry.

What the hell is he doing?

Granted, Gray had never been much of a fighter, but he did understand the basic mechanics of combat. Allowing your attacker to strike, while not defending yourself, was not something that was generally done. Gray's heart beat faster as fear for his mate consumed him. He didn't understand what was happening, but he knew that if Andreo Demos died today, Gray would follow, soon after. He couldn't survive in a world without his bossy Demon. There would be nothing left for him to live for.

When Povell's projectiles were within arm's reach of Dreo, Gray had to bite back a cry of warning. He didn't want to do anything to distract his mate, but if Dreo got himself killed, Gray was going to kick his ass. When a smile bloomed on Dreo's face, Gray had no idea what to think. He was even more confused when Dreo pursed his lips and blew out a slow, steady breath, like he was doing nothing more exciting than try to cool a bowl of hot soup.

As the stream of hot air reached the incoming missiles, Povell's hell fire began to sputter and spark, struggling to hold onto its flame. When it reached the point of actually touching Dreo, it winked out of existence completely, becoming nothing more dangerous than a gentle breeze that ruffled his mate's hair. Gray let out the breath he'd been holding, relief washing over him to see his Demon unharmed.

A quick glance at Povell showed that there might be a chink in the rogue Demon's armor. The rage was still there. The evil, too. But underneath all that, Gray could see the fear that was building inside him. It was there in his eyes, spreading like poison, infecting everything in its path. For Povell, it was the first sign of weakness. For Gray, it was a sign of hope.

Dreo was still smiling as he stared Povell down. With his muscled body standing tall and proud, and his head held high, Dreo looked like a king. A feeling of foreboding washed over him at the thought, but he ruthlessly pushed it aside. For now, he needed to be completely focused on the two of them making it through this alive. Everything else could wait.

"Was that the best you've got, old friend?" Dreo taunted. "My turn."

Dreo's attack was as different from Povell's as night is from day. Opal's, as well, was almost juvenile in comparison. There was no warning — no way to predict the strike. One minute there was nothing. The next, a wall of boiling black fire winked into existence, mere feet from Povell. It was fast moving, closing in on him in seconds. There was no time to for him avoid the attack. Only the man's Demon speed was able to save him from immediate death. Diving to take cover behind a large pile of refuse, Povell was able to avoid a direct hit, but was still struck on his left side. The furniture and other objects that Opal had previously piled up out of sheer laziness, now served to give Povell multiple points of cover. The stench of charred flesh assailed Gray's nose, causing him to force down the instinctive urge to vomit.

When Povell didn't immediately rise, Dreo began a slow approach. "Have you had enough?"

"Are you kidding?" Povell's laugh was strained. "Things are just starting to get fun." Popping up, he lobbed another round of green fire, which Dreo was easily able to evade.

"It is madness to continue this fight, Povell. If you surrender now, I will appeal to the Demon Council for leniency. Imprisonment, instead of a death sentence."

"Eternity in a cage? You've got to be joking. There is no life without freedom. Death would be a preferable fate. No. If you want to take my life, I feel it's only fair to return the favor."

Povell was on the move before Gray had time to process his words. Rolling out from behind his make-shift shelter, the Demon sprinted across the room. Even injured, he was faster that Gray's eyes could track. It left Gray feeling vulnerable, and he didn't like it.

"Dreo?"

"Stay where you are, Oracle. My men and I will keep you safe." With a nod to his Demons, they fanned out.

Povell's laugh sounded again, this time closer than before. "Is that what you think, Dreo? That you and your group of toy soldiers can protect him? What a novel idea," he sneered. "You can't even protect yourselves."

A glint of light caught Gray's eye and one of Dreo's men called out a warning. Turning, he barely had time to take in the barrage of green fire that arced toward them from behind. Even with the warning, Dreo and his men barely had time to get clear of the attack. A few of Dreo's men went down. Those who weren't injured moved in to pull their comrades out of harm's way and tend to the wounded. Dreo himself took a hit to the back while trying to cover one of his men. The power behind the hit nearly drove him to his knees. His face contorted in pain, but he never made a sound. When one of his soldiers made a move toward him, Dreo waved him off, ordering him back to help the others. Gray wanted to go to him, but stopped himself. Dreo had told him to stay where he was. He didn't want to put either of them at further risk by running out in the open, willy-nilly.

"You scurry around, hiding like vermin in a sewer," Dreo called out. "Are you afraid to face me? Where is your sense of honor?"

Povell laughed, derisively. "In case you failed to notice, *Lord Demos*, honor isn't something that holds much stock with me. Honor is a weakness. It limits you. All that truly matters is power and the ability to use it. I will always be stronger than you because there are certain places you won't go. Vulnerabilities that you won't take advantage of. Honor doesn't make you strong—it makes you a fool."

Dreo took a step forward, jaw clenched and hands fisted. "I guess we will have to agree to disagree. I am done with these games, Povell. If you want my life so bad, come and get it."

"Well, if you insist."

Gray cringed when Povell's voice sounded directly behind him, his vile breath feathering across Gray's neck. He made a move to flee but was quickly restrained by a thick arm, wrapped around his chest.

"Dreo!" Gray's cry was a warning as much as it was a cry for help.

"Release him," Dreo ordered. "Your fight is with me."

"I don't think so. You offered up your life. I've decided to take you up on that offer."

Pulling Gray in tight, Povell's mouth was at his ear. "For all that Opal is a crazy bitch, she did teach me one useful trick. Do you want to see?"

"Do I have a choice?"

Povell chuckled. "Not really." Spinning Gray around to face him, Povell placed a hand over Gray's heart. Closing his eyes, an expression of total concentration crossed the Demon's face, making Gray wonder what he was up to. The longer they stood there, locked together, the stranger Gray began to feel. At first, he assumed it was nothing more than a natural revulsion to being so close to the vile man. The sensation started in his stomach, gradually working its way up through his chest and continuing up until his head was pounding. His vision began to blur and his hands started to shake. It was when the edge of his vision became foggy, then darkened, that fear truly took over.

"The best thing about Opal," Povell whispered into his ear, "is that she knows all the secrets about Oracles. My favorite, was how to force a vision—"

Gray froze. Horror filled him at the realization of what Povell was saying. He would never have thought that Opal would have been crazy enough to tell a Demon, so completely out of his mind, an Oracle's most guarded secret. He would have thought she had some sense of self-preservation. The ability to force a vision was also the ability to make an Oracle utterly vulnerable for one moment. For most people, that amount of time was worthless. For a murderous Demon, it was all the time he needed. While teaching Balen the skill had been careless on her part, Balen was not the homicidal monster than Povell was. Giving Povell the knowledge was on par with giving a mass murderer a loaded gun with no safety, and setting him loose in a populated area. It was just a matter of time before he used it.

Looking over his shoulder, Gray sought out his mate, desperate to see him one last time. When he locked onto those dark eyes, even through the haze of an incoming vision, it felt like coming home. He smiled sadly, wishing their time together hadn't been so short. Some things were just out of their control.

"I love you!" Gray shouted as his vision faded to black. He felt the hand over his heart begin to heat through the material of his shirt and knew his end had come.

"Aw," Povell mocked. "Isn't that sweet?"

As the vision started, the weight of Povell's hand jerked away. He felt a burning pain in his heart then—

Chapter Fifteen

Gray didn't know what was happening. One minute there was a feeling of such blissful peace then the next his body was awash with pain as his ears were assailed by the sheer volume of whatever was going on around him. There were screams, shouting, an explosion off to his right—all around him, the sounds of objects crashing to the ground. None of it made any sense.

He tried to open his eyes, but his lids would not obey his commands. His body felt heavy. Almost as if he was submerged under water. When he attempted to move his arms and legs, he encountered the same feeling, like his body had been strapped down with weights. As he resigned himself to his current situation, he was startled when he felt strange hands touching him. He was jostled around briefly before he experienced a moment of weightlessness as he was lifted off the ground and carried away.

Moments, or possibly hours, later he was lowered onto a soft, cushioned surface. He was confused when someone removed his shirt, but he couldn't find the strength to truly care. All he wanted was to return to his world of peace. This world had nothing to offer him but pain and suffering.

"You do not get to leave me, Grayson Muir!"

The male voice was familiar but hard to place. It did something to him—made his insides tingle and his cock hot and needy. There were hands on him—warm, questing, familiar hands. They explored his chest, increasing the pain he felt there. He tried to pull back—escape the hurt those caused—but he was held steady.

"I'm so sorry, baby. I know it hurts, but we're trying to make it better."

The familiar voice again. He still couldn't place it, but something about that voice encouraged him to trust and obey. His muscles relaxed and his breathing calmed. Those questing hands, no longer causing pain, ran along his skin in soothing, gentle strokes. Despite the pain radiating through his chest, he still craved more of that touch. When the hand pulled away, a pitiful whine escaped his throat.

"Hush now, my mate. We'll fix this. I promise, we'll fix this." The desperate edge to the man's voice made it sound like he was trying convince himself as he much as he was trying to convince Gray. Gray didn't mind. He could listen to that voice forever and never tire of it, no matter what it was saying.

"Dreo," another voice sounded. "He's fading fast. You have to do the exchange. It's his only chance."

Dreo? He recognized that name. He tried to pull up a picture in his mind, but the effort involved was too great. For a moment, he thought he saw the hazy impression of dark eyes and a curtain of sable hair, but as he struggled to bring the figure into focus, it became more and more distorted until it finally vanished back into the darkness of his mind.

"Not without his consent," the familiar voice growled. "He has to choose it. You of all people should understand that, Maddox."

"He's not in any shape to make that choice. If you don't do it soon, there won't be anything left to save. The man is your mate. If you don't do this now, you will lose him forever."

"He'll hate me."

"Better to have him live and hate you, than let him die and you hate yourself."

The room descended into silence. For a moment, Gray thought they had left him—that they were allowing him to succumb to his fate. He started to slip away, falling back down into his world of peace. It would be so easy to just let it happen. Gray thought that knowledge would make him happy, but something about the idea of never hearing that familiar voice again bothered him deeply.

He didn't have long to examine his feelings. There were others in the room again, surrounding him. Shuffling footsteps and the scrape of objects being dragged roughly across a hard floor met his ears. A hand was on his forehead, and another brushed his bottom lip. The unexpected contact startled him, but he relaxed when he recognized that familiar touch from earlier.

"That's it, love. Relax for me," the voice soothed as fingers touched his forehead and gently brushed the hair away from Gray's eyes. If only he could see—he could put a face to that amazing voice. For reasons he didn't understand, he knew that if he could just remember this man, everything else in his world would make sense again. Unfortunately, the more he struggled to remember, the farther away the memories seemed to be.

"Gray, my love. I need you to trust me now. Can you do that for me?"

Gray knew, in his heart, that he would do anything for the man. Anything in his power, all the man had to do was ask, and it would be his. Gray tried to voice his agreement, but his vocal cords proved to be just as useless as his eyes at the moment. Thankfully, he must have managed some noise or movement of confirmation as the man, Dreo, let out a relieved breath.

"Thank you, love," Dreo breathed. "Your trust means more to me than you know. Now, I need you to drink something for me, okay? It's medicine. It's going to make you feel better—stronger. It's going to help with the pain. Are you ready?"

Again, Gray assumed he must made some noise of affirmation because before he knew it, gentle fingers were at his mouth, prying open his lips while another hand lay relaxed at his throat. Gray hadn't given much thought to the taste of the medicine he was to be given, so when the first drops landed on his tongue, he was surprised and slightly repulsed by the thick, metallic flavor that filled his mouth.

His gag reflex kicked in almost immediately. As his stomach began to heave, Gray knew there was no way he was going to be able to keep the 'medicine' down. Tears welled in his eyes and ran down his face as his stomach began to spasm and seize. Despite his struggle to keep it down, Dreo continued to drip the fluid into his mouth, massaging his throat to encourage him to swallow it down. While the taste may have been ghastly, the effects were nearly instantaneous. The effects, however, were vastly different than what Gray had expected. Instead of making Gray stronger, he felt like his insides were on fire. Before the medicine, the pain in his chest had been severe but tolerable. This was different. It was an inferno within him, boiling his blood and charring his bones. It seared through him with a force that made him wish for death. Gray struggled to lift his arms, desperate to shove away the poison that was masquerading as medicine, but the agony was too great and what little strength he'd previously had was long gone.

Why would Dreo do this to him? Gray had thought he could trust the man—believed that he could put his faith in him, only to have that faith thrown back in his face. And for what? Gray didn't understand.

The vile, noxious fluid continued to dribble into his mouth as Gray's body started to convulse. His body was consumed with tremors and still Dreo forced more of his poisonous brew down Gray's throat. Hands were on him then, strangers all around him, holding him down, allowing Dreo to do this to him. Gray wanted to fight them—to throw off their restraining hands and escape. Unfortunately, it was not to be. His strength was gone. The only escape he could hope for now was death. Damn, how he regretted not allowing himself to slip away peacefully when he'd had the chance.

Another blast of fire shot down his back, burning its way through his body like a wave of molten lava. His back arched as his spinal cord cracked and splintered under the torturous heat. The scream that escaped him proved his voice still worked if the need was great enough. Even knowing the cry came from himself, it was painful to hear. The desperate sound was torturous and heart wrenching. It was the sound of a soul pleading for mercy. Gray hoped it would haunt Dreo every night in his dreams for the rest of his extremely long life. It was no less than he deserved for such betrayal.

Desperate to face down his betrayer, Gray finally managed to crack open his eyes. What he saw was like a scene out of a war movie. The room was on fire and bodies littered the floor. Broken and bleeding, they were strewn around the room like shattered dolls. His initial horror was quelled, somewhat, when he realized that many of them were still moving. He released a sigh of relief. Injured was better than dead, any day of the week.

It was difficult to make out the rest of the room. There was a haze of smoke hanging heavy in the air from the still smoldering fires. A body to his right caught Gray's attention and had him squinting into the fog. A sudden draft of air blew through the room, disrupting the thick smog and briefly clearing the air.

As the man's face came into focus, Gray felt his chest clench and his body start to tremble, as fear and relief warred within him. With his head turned to an impossible angle and a glassy sheen in his eyes, it was clear Povell's days of torture were now over. Deep breaths, though painful, helped to calm Gary's racing heart as he soaked in the knowledge that the monster was dead.

Another wave of anguish struck him like a runaway freight train and left him gasping for air. The heat was not far behind it, striking back with a vengeance, burning through his chest, stealing all the oxygen from his lungs until Gray felt like he was inhaling fire. It scorched his airway and singed his throat. He tried to scream out his misery, but it was useless. It had finally succeeded in stealing his voice.

"Dreo! We're losing him. Finish it!"

"Fuck!"

As Gray's eyes became fixed on the stone ceiling above him, an arm appeared in his line of vision. As it moved over him, blood dripped onto his face and neck from a deep gash on its wrist. Gray didn't understand what was happening. He was fully prepared to assume it was some kind of death induced hallucination, until strong fingers once again pried open his lips, allowing that crimson spray to flow freely into his mouth and throat.

Choking and sputtering on the noxious fluid, he tried to turn his head away but was caught by strong hands that held him firmly in place. Writhing beneath those hands, he struggled in vain to escape what was being done to him. Voices sounded above him, but he wasn't able to make out their words. There was a rhythm to it, like a song or chanting. As more of the toxic fluid entered his body, he felt his strength leave him. Within minutes, even breathing became too much work. He tried to drag in one last, sawing breath, but it was useless.

His vision began to darken, no longer a warning of a vision creeping in — now, a sign of death come to claim him. As he lay on the floor, open mouthed and gasping for air, Dreo's face appeared above him. It was hard for Gray to reconcile the man he'd thought he loved with the man who was trying to kill him.

"Why?" he croaked, forcing the words out of his charred throat.

Dreo's expression was wrecked. His hair had come free from its usual queue and was hanging in a tangled mess around his shoulders. The blood, dirt and ash smudging his face did nothing to detract from his natural beauty. Even with his wide, red-rimmed eyes and clenched jaw, he was still the most gorgeous man Gray had ever seen. When Dreo reached down to cup his face, Gray couldn't hide his flinch. The look of total devastation on Dreo's face would have killed him if the blood Dreo had forced him to drink wasn't already doing that job.

"I know you don't understand, but you have to trust me." Dreo's words were pained.

Gray wanted to. God, did he want to, but Dreo was right—he didn't understand. All he knew was that Dreo had done this to him—whatever 'this' was. He wasn't sure, but it felt a lot like dying.

Spots appeared before Gray's eyes as the last of the oxygen left his lungs, then his vision went black. The room became quieter, more muffled, as he felt himself sinking back down into his blissful nothingness. It would all be over soon. The faint touch of lips on his forehead barely registered to his fading senses.

"Trust me, Gray. I won't let anything happen to you. I love you."

Gray would have laughed if he'd had the strength.

Yeah, right. Too late.

Chapter Sixteen

Gray felt strange. Maybe it was just an aftereffect of his near-death experience, but something was definitely different. The last thing he remembered, he was pretty sure he'd been dying on a cold, hard floor with Dreo, his murderer, hovering over him. Now, instead of enjoying happy hour with angels at the pearly gates, he found himself waking up alone on a small pallet in a small, dark room. In fact, if he were to guess, he'd say he was in some sort of cell. There was no art on the walls and no rich fabrics covering the bed. Besides the mattress he currently lay on, the room was completely devoid of any furniture or personal touches.

What the hell?

He wiggled his fingers and toes experimentally and was pleased when they moved without difficulty. It seemed that whatever had happened had reversed the effects of whatever Dreo had done to him. The reminder of the gorgeous man filled him with conflicting emotions of love, lust and betrayal. He still didn't understand what had happened to him but, goddamn it, he was going to find out.

Letting out a deep breath, he heaved himself up into a sitting position, instantly surprised at how little effort the movement took. He'd been expecting some pretty debilitating side effects from his ordeal, at the least. In reality, Gray couldn't remember the last time he'd felt so good. A quick inspection of his body didn't reveal any physical changes, but something was definitely different.

The sound of a throat clearing immediately grabbed his attention. As his head came up, Gray was trapped by the familiar power of an amazing set of fiery, chocolate-colored eyes. Dreo leaned against the wall by the door. His posture was relaxed, but his body language said he was anything but. His thick arms were crossed over his chest, his muscles clenched so tight his veins were standing out in stark relief. His jaw was clenched to the point of shattering. He was striking. Strong and compelling. Gray couldn't decide if he wanted to kiss him or beat the shit out of him.

"What are you doing here?" Gray hissed furiously.

Ignoring Gray's anger, Dreo took a step toward him. "How do you feel?"

"How the hell do you think I feel? You tried to kill me!"

"Never!" Dreo's response was immediate and vehement. "You are my mate. I would never hurt you. I couldn't harm you, not even if I wanted to. You are everything to me."

"Wouldn't harm me? Is that a joke?" Gray shot back bitterly. The memory of the fire and scorching pain was too much for him to dismiss so easily.

Dreo looked at him, his expression blank. "The pain was both fleeting and necessary. I am sorry for any discomfort you felt, but I will not apologize for the act itself."

"Why the hell not?" Gray yelled, enraged by Dreo's lack of remorse.

"You would have died!" Dreo snarled, his mask of cool indifference finally cracking in the face of his anger. "You were on the floor, lying in a pool of your own blood, getting ready to leave me forever. I am a selfish man, Grayson Muir. You can hate me, if you wish, but I could not let that happen. You are mine! My mate. Mine to love and mine to protect. You do not get to leave me—not ever!"

Dreo's words left Gray stunned. He'd known the Demon cared for him—they were mates after all—but he hadn't had any idea how deep the man's feelings truly went. The idea that he could inspire love in a six-hundred-year-old lust Demon, who had experienced more than Gray could ever dream of, was a little hard to believe. Judging by Dreo's look of annoyance, Gray's doubt must have been written all over his face.

Gray stared at Dreo, his gaze unwavering. He was not going to let this man intimidate him. He needed answers. "Fine. If you want me to believe that you weren't trying to kill me, then what the hell happened? What did you do to me?"

Dreo let out a weary sigh and ran a hand through his still tousled locks. "Demons and Shifters are a lot alike, when it comes to mating. When mates wish to officially join, there is a ceremony where vows are exchanged. Promises of love and loyalty are made. There are even protection spells cast over them to help keep the couple, and their love, safe from harm. The final step is the blood exchange."

"Excuse me?" Gray sputtered. "The blood what?" His voice had risen to an embarrassing level, but there was no help for it.

"The blood exchange," Dreo repeated slowly, like he was speaking to a child. The scowl on his face made it clear that he was not happy with Gray's response. "For Shifters, it's done with a bite. Deep enough to draw blood and scar, their main focus is essentially marking their territory and warning others to stay away.

"Demons are different. The exchange of blood is everything. It is not a symbolic gesture, but a true sharing of the mind, body and spirit. It connects us. By allowing our mates to ingest our blood, we give them access to the very thing that makes us who we are. The exchange makes us stronger, faster and speeds up our ability to heal. It is also the final step in the mating process." Dreo sighed. "You were dying. The one hope I had, was the possibility that the accelerated healing that came with the exchange would be enough to repair the damage Povell's blast had inflicted. It is the only reason that I did what I did. I had no other choice."

Gray was embarrassed to admit that it took him a minute to realize what Dreo was telling him. "So, you're trying to tell me that the only way to save me, was to give me blood — your blood?"

"Yes." Dreo frowned, but Gray didn't think that it was directed at him.

"Okay. I think I get it. I've got to admit, I'm a little bit grossed out with the whole ingesting of bodily fluids thing, but I understand why it was necessary. Now, tell me, why do you look so upset?"

"It was too soon," Dreo growled, his expression dark. "I wanted to wait until I was sure."

Gray sucked in a sharp, painful breath. Dreo's words were like a punch in the gut. With his own feelings for the other man growing so strong, so fast, he had assumed Dreo's were the same.

"I guess you're right," Gray replied, dismissively. He moved to take a step back, needing to distance himself from the man who both held his heart and was breaking it. "We probably shouldn't have rushed into anything. I mean, just because we're mates, doesn't mean we have to be together."

Dreo's eyes narrowed dangerously. "Be careful what you say, Oracle. You wouldn't want me to start believing any of that bullshit coming out of your mouth. Especially if you don't want to spend the next month chained to my bed, proving who you belong to." His raised brow dared Gray to question of the seriousness of his words.

"Fine," Gray huffed petulantly, crossing his arms over his chest. "Explain it to me then."

Dreo rolled his eyes, his irritation abundantly clear. "In some cases, the blood exchange can have an additional side effect. There have been a few isolated instances where the exchange has led to the development of new powers."

Gray shook his head. "I don't understand. New powers? How is that even possible?"

"I wish I had an answer for you. To be honest, we're not really sure. There are many theories, but the appearance of additional gifts seems to be pretty random."

"Okay—so, what's the problem?"

Dreo sighed. "From what we've been able to ascertain, while the onset of abilities seems to vary, abilities are more likely to appear in mates with some type of para in their family tree. Something in the genetics seems to make them more susceptible. While they are all affected in some ways, there are a few species of para that have been found to be affected more strongly than the others. The effects have been — unpredictable."

"Unpredictable?"

"Unstable — dangerous, even."

Brows furrowed, Gray frowned. "What does that have to do with me?"

"Don't play dumb, Gray. I told you, there is para in your family — there has to be. Either one or both of your parents. There has never been an Oracle born to pure human parents and I don't believe you are going to be the first." Dreo cocked his head, considering. "There is something…more about you. It's something that goes even beyond your being an Oracle. With my suspicions and our lack of knowledge about your heritage, I wasn't willing to risk the blood exchange. I wanted more time to investigate — to make sure that you wouldn't be in any danger before we attempted it. Unfortunately" — he grimaced — "that choice has been taken out of our hands."

"But, I'm going to be fine…right?"

Dreo gave him a worried look. "For now. We still need to track down as much information about your birth family as we can. I don't want there to be any unfortunate surprises down the road that we aren't prepared for."

"All right, so it's done and there's no going back," Gray reasoned. "What does that mean for me — for us?"

"I don't know," Dreo answered, his eyes softening in concern. "I've never heard of a blood exchange like ours. Definitely never one completed under such circumstances. The pain, nearly dying… It shouldn't have happened that way. I would never have wanted you to suffer like that." Dreo reached out, cupping Gray's jaw gently, like he was something precious that needed to be handled with extreme care. "That pain should have been mine to bear."

Gray pushed away his hand, lips pursed in irritation. "Don't treat me like some damsel in distress, Dreo. I'm strong. I don't need you to protect me." When Dreo's brow arched, Gray scowled. "All right, asshole. I needed you to rescue me before, but that was just a one-time thing. I'm usually pretty good a taking care of myself. Ask anyone."

Dreo laughed, brushing a stand of hair away from Gray's face. "It doesn't matter. You are my mate. Caring for you is my purpose in life. The sooner you accept that, the better."

Gray frowned but didn't respond, knowing it would be useless to argue with the infuriating man. His Demon was the most stubborn person he had ever met. Gray could relate—he probably came in a close second. "How about we look out for each other?" He studiously ignored Dreo's knowing smirk, as well as the flush that was working its way up his neck.

Man, is it getting hot, or what?

Shaking his head, Gray tried to rein in his rampant thoughts. "All right," he muttered, clearing his throat, "now that we've got that settled, can you explain to me why the hell I'm waking up in a jail cell?"

Dreo looked away, but not before Gray caught a hint of nervousness on his face. "It was—safer—to keep you somewhere a little more contained." Gray knew there was more to Dreo's words when his lover wouldn't meet his eyes.

"What do you mean by 'safer'?"

Dreo blew out a breath. "After you blacked out, I placed you in our bed so I could care for you while we waited for—"

Gray coughed, his brows practically disappeared into his hairline, causing Dreo to pause.

"Yeah, that's right, I said *our* bed, you cocky piece of shit. It's the truth, so stop being such a dick about it." Dreo shot him a dark scowl before continuing. "I had called for healers to examine you to ensure you were not in need of further treatment. They had finished their examination and were on their way out, when one of the senior healers mentioned that they had forgotten to get a blood sample. One of his apprentices was sent back to extract a vial for testing."

Gray must have made a noise of protest because Dreo already had a hand raised to calm him. "Easy, sweetheart. There was nothing nefarious about the request and I was present the entire time. Besides"— he chuckled—"after today, I don't think you'll have to worry about them coming anywhere near you without advance permission."

"Huh?"

Dreo's smile softened. "I believe we witnessed the first manifestation of your new powers." When Gray's confusion didn't diminish, Dreo chuckled. "When the healer moved in to draw blood, a shrill screech pierced the air, the bed began to shake then all the pillows from the bed rose into the air and began chasing the poor man around the room. They circled around him like a flock of seagulls on a sandwich, smacking him in the head, before dive bombing him and scaring him half to death. And the whole time you just lay there, still as a stone, looking like a goddamn angel."

Gray couldn't believe what he was hearing. His face flushed with embarrassment. "Are you kidding?"

"Not at all. Telekinesis is not a common gift, for Demons or other paras. It was a truly amazing sight to see. If you are able to learn to control it, it will be a very powerful talent."

"Easy for you to say." Gray glowered, crossing his arms over his chest defensively. "You're not the one who attacked someone while unconscious—even though he did deserve it for trying to take my blood without my permission. That better not happen again." He scowled at Dreo, hoping his mate understood his words for the threat they were. Gray could not be held responsible for his actions if anyone tried a stunt like that again. He wasn't giving any further warnings on the matter.

"Sweetheart, don't be upset. I can promise you that it will never happen again," Dreo murmured, softly. "After the shock you gave the healers, I wouldn't be surprised if they started asking you permission before they used the restroom. No way in hell do any of them want to be on your bad side, my fierce mate."

Reaching over, Dreo pulled Gray into his arms, holding him to his chest, pressed snug against his heart. Dreo's breath ruffled his hair, effectively calming him in a way nothing else ever had. Gray sagged in his arms, just taking a minute to breath in the scent of his mate. The scent of dark chocolate, burning wood and cinnamon had Gray's mouth watering for a taste. The gentle press of lips at his temple had him fighting back a smile.

"Telekinesis, huh? So, that's like being able to move shit with my mind, right?"

Dreo smiled against his temple. "Simply put, yes. You can move *shit* with your mind."

"And the reason I am waking up in a cell—?"

"There's less ammunition down here. I wasn't sure who else you might decide annoyed you enough to attack. Some I couldn't care less about, but others are valuable members of the court that I would prefer to keep around. I decided to err on the side of caution. Better safe than sorry."

Gray tried to look offended by the accusation but failed miserably. He was just too happy to be alive. There was no way to contain his smile. Tilting his head, Gray flashed a playful look over his shoulder. "Hmm—able to move things with my mind—that could be fun. Just imagine the possibilities." Licking his lips, he wiggled his brows suggestively, eliciting another chuckle from his Demon.

"I do believe you will keep me on my toes, my Oracle."

Gray leered. "My current plans have less to do with your toes, and more to do with your naked body, riding my ass like you own it. Think you're up to the challenge?"

Dreo's eyes darkened, their normal creamy brown fading out until it was almost impossible to distinguish where the iris ended and the pupil began. The last bit of color left was from the flickering flames of hellfire that had begun to smolder in their inky depths. The sight of those lethal flames had Gray's cock jerking to attention so fast he would have thought it was on fire.

With all his blood rushing south, Gray fought back a moment of dizziness. Reaching out, he grabbed a hold of Dreo's rock hard shoulder in an effort to steady himself. Muscles clenched beneath his fingers and sinew tightened to the point it was like stone under his hand. Glancing up, Gray found himself trapped by the power of Dreo's intense scrutiny. With his jaw clenched tight and his eyes in full flame, he looked like a wild animal on the verge of attack. In Gray's eyes, the man had never been more gorgeous. Call him an idiot, but he was more than willing to help tame that beast. He could already feel the heat starting to build within him.

"Oracle…"

Dreo's guttural moan just about brought Gray to his knees. "Mate," Gray whimpered. He knew he sounded pitiful, but his need had grown too great for him to care. He was two seconds from stripping naked, spreading himself open and presenting his backside like a dog in heat. He needed to be filled, needed to be taken, and there was only one man up to the task and all it entailed.

"You are in need?"

"Yes," Gray hissed, as his stomach cramped, his breath coming in wheezing gasps.

"What do you need?"

"You—just you."

"You're goddamned right!" The words had no more left Dreo's lips and he was on him, his eyes brimming with carnal intent. Gray had a moment of apprehension until he remembered that this loss of control was what he wanted. He didn't need soft, gentle touches. He needed to be claimed—owned—by this powerful man, and he couldn't wait another minute.

"Strip," Gray demanded, barely managing to break away from Dreo's devouring mouth.

Dreo snarled. "No. Need to get you back to our room—need a bed—"

"No!" Gray's cry was desperate. "I need you now!" Shoving back, his quick movement surprised Dreo into loosening his grip, giving him the opportunity to dash for the opposite side of the room. Not wanting to waste time, Gray quickly peeled off his shirt and began to work of the fastenings of his pants. In seconds, he had them shucked down past his knees and pooled around his ankles. Bracing his hands against the wall and canting his hips, Gray presented his ass for Dreo's inspection. He knew he must look like some wanton slut, but he didn't care. He had almost died, and now, he needed his mate to show him that he was still alive.

"Fuck me," he groaned, the words jumbled together in a garbled mess.

When Dreo didn't move, Gray pushed his butt out as far as he manage without falling and wiggled his ass, further exposing himself to his Demon's hungry gaze. A soft breeze skated across his skin, teasing his entrance, moments before rough hands took rounded globes in a bruising grip. His cheeks were given a firm squeeze before Dreo pried them open farther, giving him unrestricted access to Gray's gaping hole. A thick finger tickled his entrance, causing Gray to shudder and squirm in need

"Look at you," Dreo snarled, running a hot hand down Gray's right cheek and flank. "Butt out, legs spread wide, asshole just begging to be filled... Is that what you want? You want someone to shove a big cock in that hungry ass of yours? Fill you up until you feel like you're gonna burst? Until you think you're gonna split in half?"

Gray loved when Dreo talked dirty to him when they fucked. It was like the man had a direct line to his libido through his words. Gray's brain fogged and his imagination went wild as he began to envision every act Dreo described. His cock hardened to the point of pain, making it impossible for Gray to focus on anything other than his burgeoning arousal. When Dreo's hand cracked down on his ass, he jolted, completely taken by surprise.

"I asked you a question," Dreo growled. "Don't make me repeat myself."

"Yes," Gray panted. "God, yes."

"Are you telling me just any dick will do? That anyone with a big, thick cock is welcome to shove it up that tight chute of yours?"

"No!" Gray's shout echoed off the walls. "Just you! Nobody but you!"

Dreo's lips twisted into a satisfied smirk. "You better fucking believe it. This is my ass. Mine to fill, mine to fuck. Nobody else will ever touch you here again."

Gray nodded his head vehemently. His arousal was so great, he was past the point of coherent words. The whines and whimpers coming out of his mouth would surely haunt him forever, once his head cleared, but for now, they didn't matter. The only thing that mattered was getting his mate inside him.

Dreo dropped to his knees behind him, still maintaining a firm grip on his cheeks. Warm breath skimmed his hole, followed by the hot, wet stroke of Dreo's questing tongue. He teased and tickled around the edge of Gray's entrance, causing his asshole to clench and release sporadically. Soft licks, followed by sharp nibs to his sensitive flesh, drove Gray to the brink of madness. Dreo kept him riding the edge, so close to release, but always just beyond reach. His vision blurred, as moisture filled his eyes.

"Dreo," Gray cried, the tears breaking free and streaming down his face. "Please."

"Soon." Without warning, Dreo pointed his tongue and speared it into Gray's vulnerable hole. Stroke after stroke—deeper and deeper—he thrust, reaching new depths within Gray's body. Dreo pushed his face farther into Gray's crack which, in turn, shoved Gray harder into the wall. The cold stone against his hard cock was both painful and arousing. Unable to control himself, Gray began to thrust his hips, systematically humping forward against the wall, then fucking himself back on Dreo's thick tongue. His need for release was now a continuous mantra, beating away in his brain.

Tingling at the base of his spine and the tightening of his balls signaled the approach of Gray's long-awaited climax. He was just feeling the first tendrils of ecstasy creep over him when Dreo ripped himself away. Gray cried out, the denial of completion too much for him to take in silence.

There was a rustling of cloth then Dreo was back, his hard, muscled body pressed tight against Gray's sweat slicked back. The hard rod of his arousal rode Gray's crack, a small tease of what was to come. Strong arms were wrapped around him from behind, holding him steady and effectively trapping him against the unforgiving wall. Dreo brought one hand up to play with his nipples, using his agile fingers to pinch, tug and tease them into red, swollen points. Dreo slid his other hand down his abdomen, following the dark line of hair below his navel until it reached the spot Gray needed it most. Dreo took his cock in hand, wrapping his long fingers around Gray's arousal, giving it a few hard pumps. Gray moaned. He loved the feel of Dreo's rough, calloused hand on the sensitive skin of his dick. The tiny licks of pain when the skin caught practically sent him into orbit. Pushing forward, he shoved his dick farther into Dreo's fist.

"Are you ready for me, Oracle?" Dreo growled, licking a wet path up the side of his neck. "Ready to take my fat cock deep inside you? It's amazing how tight you are. Gonna stretch you wide and make you mine."

"Please," Gray whined.

Dreo barked out a laugh. "I love it when you beg. I'm gonna fuck you hard and fill you with my cum until you're dripping with it. Gonna mark you from the inside out, so that no one will doubt who you belong to."

Without further warning, Dreo released Gray's dick, pulled his cheeks wide, lined up the blunt head of his weeping cock and thrust. He didn't stop until he was balls deep in Gray's backside. Gray groaned and squirmed, the contrast from being so empty to being filled past capacity in mere seconds had him fighting to keep conscious, even as blackness teased the edge of his vision. He had waited too long to allow unconsciousness to rob him of the pleasure to come. Taking a few calming breaths, Gray finally began to relax around Dreo's invading flesh.

Dreo waited, a fact that Gray was eternally grateful for, until a nod of approval from Gray spurred him into motion. Once unleashed, there was no holding back, as evidenced by the hard, driving rhythm Dreo started as he fucked Gray with a force he'd never experienced before. After pulling nearly free of Gray's sheath, he then shoved his entire length back into Gray in one, brutal thrust, leaving him gasping for air and moaning in pleasure.

"You like that, don't you?" Dreo's gravelly voice at his ear sent a shiver down Gray's spine. "You like it rough. Love it when I use you hard and leave you aching when I'm done, don't you? Don't you?" Dreo punctuated his questions with a series of hammering thrusts.

"Yes," Gray groaned, pushing back against his harsh strokes. "I love it. Fuck me hard—use me—make me feel it."

"Oh, you'll feel it, all right," Dreo snarled. "By the time I'm done with you, your ass is going to be feeling me for weeks. I'm going to fuck you until you can't walk, and then I'm going to fuck you more. When I'm finished, you're gonna forget what it feels like to not have my cock filling you."

"Oh, God."

"Not God. Dreo."

Taking a step back, Dreo pulled out of Gray, causing him to cry out. The move left his hole open and grasping. The feeling of emptiness was almost more than Gray could bear. Before he had a chance to voice his disapproval, Dreo had a hand on his arm and jerked him around. Now face to face, Gray's breath caught as he saw the wild ferocity in his mate's eyes. Dreo pressed their groins together in a wet, sticky mess of cock on cock. Grabbing Gray's butt in his hands, Dreo hoisted him up against the wall, tilting his hips before thrusting his swollen dick back into Gray's empty passage.

"You feel so fucking good," Dreo groaned against Gray's neck. "So tight and hot."

"Harder," Gray gasped. "Fuck me harder."

Shifting his grip, Dreo grabbed the back of Gray's legs and shoved his knees up to his chest. The move had Gray damn near bent in half. It also gave Dreo a new angle and made it possible for him to get even deeper inside Gray, reaching previously untouched depths within him. With the new angle, Gray swore he could practically feel Dreo's cock tickling the back of his throat.

"Yeah, that's it," Dreo growled. "You've got all of me now. Squeezing me so tight. Fucking perfect."

Dreo's words, combined with the hard thrusts against his abused bottom, pushed Gray past the point of no return. The tingling in his spine was back and he knew there would be no stopping it this time.

"Dreo—gonna come," he panted, forcing the words out of his gasping lips.

"Do it," Dreo ordered. "I want to feel your ass tighten around my dick like a vise. Want to see you paint our chests with your cum. Fucking do it!"

Gray was helpless to disobey. Dreo's harsh order was just what he needed to send him careening over the edge into oblivion. Lights flashed behind his eyes and he was pulled into a climax so powerful, it was almost painful. Cum shot from his dick, the force behind it so strong, the spray reached up his neck and grazed the side of his face. His channel clenched, constricting tightly around Dreo's cock and dragging him into climax as well. Never stopping in his rutting, Dreo's roar shook the room as Gray's insides were awash in the scalding heat. The sensation of his mate emptying his release inside Gray's body made him feel complete. Stream after stream fired against the walls of his chute in a seemingly endless torrent. Moisture wet the inside of his thighs as Dreo's release overflowed from his depths.

Even as their climax began to ebb, Dreo stayed inside Gray, keeping them joined as the last of the aftershocks continued to work their way through their bodies. They were finally forced to separate when Dreo's softening cock slipped free of Gray's still grasping channel, eliciting a moan from them both.

Lowering his legs back down to the floor, Gray appreciated the fact that Dreo made sure he was steady before taking a step back. As he took in Gray's appearance, Dreo's gaze heated.

"That is so fucking hot. Look at you — so full of my seed that you're dripping with it. Damn! It makes me tempted to leave you like this — sweat slick body, well fucked expression, gaping asshole still dripping with my cum. Nobody would doubt that you were mine if they saw you like this."

Gray whimpered, not sure if he was repulsed by the idea or turned on. Dreo merely smirked at his response. "Don't worry, sweetheart. This body is for my eyes alone. I will be the only one who gets the benefit of seeing your lust-blown eyes and kiss-swollen lips. I suppose I will just have to find another way of showing everyone who you belong to."

"Whatever you say," Gray answered dismissively, trying to calm his racing heart. "As long as it doesn't involve wearing your bodily fluids, I'm willing to consider it."

Dreo chuckled, walking over to their pile of discarded clothes. He handed Gray his pants and shirt, before starting to pull on his own. "No. No bodily fluids, but you'll definitely need to wear something of mine. I do need to stake my claim, after all. No, I was thinking more along the lines of a ring." Dreo arched a questioning brow.

"A r-ring?" Gray stammered, shock making speech more difficult than it should have been. "What kind of ring?"

"This kind." Dreo reached into his pocket and pulled out a small metal box. Holding it out to Gray, he lifted the lid, revealing a round band made of what appeared to be molded amber.

"What is — ?"

"The ring is made of a special substance called *democilotite*. Believe it or not, it starts out as ordinary stone. Every Demon is charged with choosing their own. Once chosen, the mineral is then heated and formed while in the midst of a Demon's hellfire. It is customary that when a Demon meets their true mate, they create such a band as a token of their devotion."

"You mean, you made this...for me?"

Dreo smiled. "Yes. Every Demon makes their mate's ring from their own hellfire. The stone is able to absorb some of our magic from the fire, imbibing it with additional spells of protection."

Reaching out, Gray hesitantly ran a finger over the smooth surface of the band. "So, what you're actually saying is that, by allowing it to form within your hellfire and absorb elements of your magic, this ring is literally a piece of you? You are giving me a piece of yourself?"

Smiling wider, Dreo cupped Gray's cheek. "Yes."

Gray sucked in a breath. "Wow. I've got to say — best gift ever."

"So, Grayson Muir," Dreo murmured, holding out the box as an offering to Gray, "will you accept my ring, as a sign of our mating and love?"

Gray's eyes widened comically. "Are you kidding?" Reaching out a hand with near blinding speed, Gray grabbed the ring from the box and jammed in onto his finger. "You had better believe I'm accepting it. If you think you're ever getting this back, you'll have to prying it off my cold, dead finger. You're stuck with me, so you better just get used to it."

The smile that formed on Dreo's face practically lit the whole room. "I'm sure I can find a way to come to terms with it."

"Good," Gray retorted gruffly, his throat thick with emotion. "Don't think this gets you out of making it official, though. I fully expect a bonding ceremony, with all of our friends there to witness you making an honest man out of me. If I don't have visual proof, nobody is going to believe it."

Laughing, Dreo pulled Gray into his arms. "An event where I get to show everyone that you truly do belong to me — mind, body, and soul? I think I can manage that."

Snuggling in deeper to Dreo's embrace, Gray sighed, loving the feel of his mate's arms wrapped around him. "So," he murmured sleepily, "what else happened after I passed out? Is it safe to assume that Opal and Povell have been dealt with?"

Dreo's arm tightened around him, then relaxed. "Yes," Dreo growled menacingly. "They have both been dealt with, although much more mercifully than either of them deserved. Neither will be able to hurt you, ever again."

"Opal?"

"It was a struggle but Balen was able to defeat her. Being a much better man that I, he gave her a chance to surrender with her life. I'm pleased to say that she declined his offer and he gifted her with true death."

Gray couldn't say he was sorry about that. She had been a murderous bitch.

"I guess that ends her bid at Queen of the Underworld."

Dreo chuckled. "I does indeed. I have news on that front, if you're interested."

Gray froze. "Please tell me they didn't make you Lord of the Underworld. I cannot be Queen of the Underworld. I mean, I could, but I really, really don't want to." Screwing up his face and sticking out his lip,

Gray knew he probably looked like a petulant child, but there was no way he wanted to be trapped in Hell. Sarah would never forgive him, or herself, for wishing him there so many times if he actually ended up having to stay there forever.

Dreo's smile grew wider. "No, my mate. I can happily assure you that I am not going to be the next Lord. Actually, Balen has been offered the position. Between his assistance with the investigation and his personal connection to the last Lord, the Elders believe he is the best choice. It is a decision I agree with, whole-heartedly."

"And what of his initial involvement?"

"He had no involvement with the death of Lucifer. His only crime was a need to make his father accountable for a perceived wrong. It was a family matter that I do not believe needs to be brought to the Elders' attention."

Gray nodded. "Balen will be a good Lord. He just needs to believe in himself."

"Agreed."

"And Povell?"

"Povell met a similar end to Opal."

"Care to elaborate?" Gray raised a questioning brow.

"Not particularly." Dreo's evasiveness immediately put Gray on alert. The words were said carelessly, but it didn't take a genius to see that Dreo was hiding something.

"Dreo…" Gray wanted answers, and his tone brooked no argument.

Dreo scowled. "Fine. When Povell blasted you, I may have been a bit…put out."

"What the heck does that mean?"

"It means that I was pissed off, Gray. I saw you go down, my power surged in response, I went after him and I kind of broke his neck."

"How do you 'kind of' break someone's neck?" Gray's voice reached an octave he'd never managed before, and hoped he never would again.

"It may have been closer to decapitation, if you want to be all technical about it." Gray's mouth dropped open in shock and Dreo scowled. "What do you want me to say, Gray? The asshole tried to kill my mate. If you want me to apologize, then you better not hold your breath because it's not going to happen. I would do it again, in a second. That bastard is going to spend all of eternity suffering in the Pits, as he deserves. I have no regrets."

Gray would have teased him for his vehemence if he hadn't seen the emotion brimming in his eyes. He had no room to judge. If their situations had been reversed, Gray would have done the exact same thing. Cupping Dreo's jaw between his hands, Gray brought him down into a kiss that he hoped conveyed all the love and adoration he felt for his man. When they separated, Gray was pleased to see the slightly dazed expression on his Demon's face.

"You have nothing to apologize for, Andreo Demos. Not one fucking thing."

Dreo's eyes widened and, for a moment, he looked stunned. Slowly, a smile formed on his lips and his eyes began to shine, not with the glow of hellfire, but with happiness.

"I love you, Grayson Muir."

"What can I say? I'm easy to love. I don't know if anyone's told you, but I'm kind of a big deal. You know, me being The Oracle and all." Gray smirked and brushed off a shoulder.

"Gray," Dreo growled, playful, pinching him in the thigh.

"All right, all right already. Stop with the boney, pinchy fingers—I bruise easily. Of course I love you, too. Honestly? Was there ever any doubt?"

It was Dreo's turn to smirk. "Not really. You were just fighting fate there, at the beginning. I knew I'd wear you down eventually. I grow on people."

"Yeah," Gray muttered, quietly, "like a fungus."

"Hey! I heard that." Dreo was trying for offended, but Gray could sense his underlying mirth. "I have a feel that with you in my life, things will never be boring."

"Is that a problem?" Gray raised a questioning brow.

"Hell, no." Dreo smiled. "I wouldn't have it any other way."

About the Author

Born and raised in Western Michigan, JJ Black's love affair with books started young and has only grown with age. Always a fan of supernatural fiction and romance, JJ stumbled across the M/M genre and has never looked back.

JJ Black loves to hear from readers. You can find her contact information, website details and author profile page at http://www.totallybound.com.

Totally Bound Publishing